Praise for

WINNER
Coventry Inspiration Book Award

SHORTLISTED
Waterstone's Children's Book Prize
UK Literary Association Book Award
Brilliant Book Award
Heart of Harwick Children's Book Award
Sefton Super Reads Award
Waverton Good Read Children's Award

NOMINATED
CILIP Carnegie Medal

"Exceptional"
Lancashire Evening Post

"Beautifully told ... moving"
tBk Magazine

Ruth Eastham was born in Lancashire, England, and trained as a teacher in Cambridge. She has since worked in more than a dozen different schools in the UK, New Zealand, Australia and Italy. Her first novel, *The Memory Cage*, won the Coventry Inspiration Book Award and has been shortlisted for numerous national and regional awards. *The Messenger Bird* is her second novel.

www.rutheastham.com
www.twitter.com/RuthEastham1

THE
MESSENGER
BIRD

RUTH EASTHAM

■SCHOLASTIC

for Max, Anna and Elena

KSYOE KUZHZ ZAUOG HBF

First published in the UK in 2012 by Scholastic Children's Books
An imprint of Scholastic Ltd
Euston House, 24 Eversholt Street
London, NW1 1DB, UK
Registered office: Westfield Road, Southam, Warwickshire, CV47 0RA
SCHOLASTIC and associated logos are trademarks and/or
registered trademarks of Scholastic Inc.

Text copyright © Ruth Eastham, 2012
The right of Ruth Eastham to be identified as the author
of this work have been asserted by her.

ISBN 978 1407 12461 2

A CIP catalogue record for this book
is available from the British Library.

Printed and bound by CPI Group (UK) Ltd, Croydon, CR0 4YY
Papers used by Scholastic Children's Books are made from
wood grown in sustainable forests.

1 3 5 7 9 10 8 6 4 2

www.scholastic.co.uk/zone

"We believe the target areas will be . . . probably in the vicinity of London, but if further information indicates Coventry, Birmingham or elsewhere, we hope to get instructions out in time."

RAF to Winston Churchill & Commands,
the morning of 14 November, 1940
National Archives AIR 2/5238

1
Plot Night

I didn't notice the men at first.

Dad was late so Mum had got the bonfire going and the flames had already set fire to the guy's ripped jeans and the wisps of straw sticking out from its charity-shop jumper. It sat on a perch of piled-up wood with its grinning plastic mask, Dad's old tie dangling round its neck like a noose.

The smells of smoke and sausages and singed baked potatoes wafted about in the cold air, making my mouth water. Mum and my big sister, Hannah, stood behind a table at the other end of our huge garden, dishing up hot chocolate and cake to practically the whole village. I picked the people out in the bonfire light while I munched toffee from a paper bag — a group who worked at the hospital where Mum's a nurse; a few of Hannah's sixth-form college friends off her journalism course; my best mates, Sasha and Josh, grabbing food. I smiled to myself as Josh's paper plate collapsed, sending him sprawling to catch rolling cakes, and Sasha bending forward with the giggles.

That's when I saw the two men. I wondered who they were, standing side by side in long, dark coats, hats pulled low, covering their faces.

"Welcome, everyone, to our new home!" Mum called over the crackling fire.

"Bit of a cold night for a house-warming, isn't it?" someone shouted, and everyone laughed. Everyone except those two blokes, the miserable things.

I pulled my scarf tighter. Everything was always late in our family. It had taken us months to get around to having a house-warming party for big old Foxglove Cottage, which we'd inherited off Great-Auntie Hilda, together with her dog and all her Second World War junk. Then Dad'd had the idea to combine the house-warming with a Bonfire Night party, which he said was symbolic. Hannah had said yes, it was symbolic of being a cheapskate, but why worry if *Remember, remember, the tenth of November* didn't have quite the same ring to it, and while we were at it why not celebrate Nathan's birthday as well since it was only three days away. But Dad had given me a wink and said there'd be something extra special all of its own for my birthday, because it's not every day that you turn thirteen.

Where *was* Dad? I stared round the garden. Mum had roped Sasha's dad into doing the fireworks, and he was

2

getting ready to set them off, which didn't really go with his posh accountant's coat. I didn't want them to start yet. Dad and I always watched the fireworks together.

A cheer went up as flames burst over the guy.

"Here, Nat."

Dad was back at last! He handed me a lit sparkler, his warm hand over mine. Stars splashed from the sparkler's tip like a magic wand. He had one too and I felt my mouth crack open in a grin and together we wrote our names fast in the air: NATHAN – LEON. LEON – NATHAN. Then round and round we went in a faster and faster, brighter and brighter, fizzing, spinning eye that was still there when I blinked.

I laughed and looked up into Dad's face and he smiled at me, but I saw he was out of breath, and there were dark circles under his eyes. He'd been at work a lot recently. Back late from his commute to London. Too many deadlines. I squeezed his arm and chewed more toffee, the chunks bunging up my mouth like sweet cement. A rocket whizzed up. It sprayed coloured light against the nearly full moon with a gunshot thud. Glowing straw floated through the air as the guy's mask sizzled and melted away.

I glanced across at the two men. They seemed to be staring in our direction. Dad was looking at them too, the sparkler a spitting stump in his hand, and his face had gone all serious and I felt my heartbeat speed up. I looked at the men more closely, at their coats and their hats and the gloved hands curled in fists at their sides. There was something weird about the way they were standing there, not moving. Just watching. Watching us?

"Dad," I managed. "Who are those. . ."

"I thought I had more time," Dad muttered to himself, cutting me off. He stood with his back to the bonfire so he glowed all around the edges. He came close to my ear. "Nat, I've got to tell you something. Something important."

I smirked. "Taping our conversation, are you, Dad?" I chomped, my mouth still full of the toffee, because that's what Dad did, on his flash new touch-screen phone. Taped all his conversations, like he was 007 or someone. He might have a desk job at the Ministry of Defence, but if you asked me he took the Special Services stuff a bit too far.

"This isn't a game, Nat." I stopped smiling. Dad's face had gone an ashy colour, like he was ill. "I've run out of time."

The men were moving towards us now, through the clumps of people, and Dad was tracking them out of the corner of his eye, but he didn't turn his head and he was speaking very low and very fast. "You've got to follow Lily's trail, Nat. Without evidence we've got nothing." His eyes glistened in the light from the bonfire. "Follow Lily's trail. She lived in this house." He had hold of my arm. "Promise me, Nat. Please. You won't have long. I'm sorry to put you through this. I should have told you things before. . ." I felt his fingernails digging into me. "I found something out. It has to be our secret. Promise me."

But I couldn't say anything back because my jaw was stuck together with the toffee, so I just nodded like an idiot.

"Don't tell anyone either, Nat, I need you to promise that as well. Not even your mum or Hannah. The more people who know, the more dangerous it is. You can't trust anyone else either, you hear me? Don't trust anyone."

I breathed fast in the bitter air. "OK," I spluttered. "But what's going on?"

"I'm innocent, Nat. Remember that."

Somewhere nearby a little kid was crying. The frosty grass made shadows like teeth in the moonlight. The men were close now; too close to say more.

"And you'd better do your history homework, Nathan!" Dad let out a loud bellow of a laugh, but his eyes were boring into me. "Don't ruddy try and hide it like you did the last time!"

He shot me a look and I stared at him, forcing down the stupid toffee. Dad never calls me Nathan. And he never swears at me. Never.

But I didn't get a chance to say anything back because then the men were between me and Dad, talking to him, but I couldn't hear over the firework bangs. One had hold of Dad's arm. I tried to get closer, but they pressed me away. Both of them had hold of Dad now and I pushed forward to get to him but he shook his head at me. He let them lead him off as if he accepted it. I followed, stumbling on half-eaten toffee apples and plastic cups dropped in the mud. Nobody seemed to be noticing anything, only the exploding fireworks, and I wanted to shout for help, shout for Mum, but all I could do was try and keep up with Dad and the two men.

People gasped and as I glanced back I saw the bonfire rise up and the guy collapse into the flames. I got round to the front of the house, out of sight of the party, and the men pushed Dad into a waiting car as the engine revved.

For a tiny second our eyes met and I saw the secret message there. *Remember*, Dad was saying. *Remember what I said.*

There were sounds of laughing and clapping from the garden. The door slammed and it had tinted glass so I couldn't see in, and the car lurched off fast down the lane, sending beams into the sky like searchlights, and my throat was all squeezed tight with panic like I was going to choke.

And Dad was gone.

2

The First Clue

I watched the moonlight creep over the frosty garden towards our house. 23:50, my alarm clock said, nearly midnight, but there was no way I could sleep and I hadn't even bothered getting ready for bed when Mum left. When would she be back from the police headquarters? She'd been away hours. Hannah was left in charge, but she'd gone off to her room with hardly a word. I'd just been sitting in the dark, waiting. Sitting, waiting. Why didn't Mum ring?

I'd tried phoning her mobile, but it was always engaged. I'd even dialled Dad's number just to see, but all I got was a continuous, dead tone and I guessed they'd made him switch it off.

I rested my elbows on the window ledge and looked out at the mess of plastic cups and firework casings over the silvery lawn, and the circle of ash where the bonfire had been. Beyond was the old well with its broken roof, and the tool shed. At the edge of the woods was a dark, humped shape, the crumbling air-raid shelter Auntie Hilda had wanted Dad to fix. Over the trees, stars glinted like bits of broken glass. I could hear Hannah's muffled voice in her bedroom through the wall, probably on her mobile to her boyfriend, Gavin.

Fireworks sounded in the distance. My insides shrank. I saw Dad being pushed into that car with tinted windows. The image was like a piece of a film I didn't want to watch, but it just kept rewinding and replaying, over and over. Why had they taken him? What did they think he'd done?

Was it something to do with his work at the Ministry of Defence? A team of government officials came to search the house as soon as Mum managed to break the party up. Didn't waste any time. Special Services people in dark clothes and dark gloves. A couple of them had the "MoD" emblem on their coats – the crown and the anchor and the eagle with its wings spread. They were all over, looking in every room, every drawer, every cupboard, ignoring every single one of Mum's questions. I'd watched them take Dad's computer and all the paperwork from his study. They'd reminded me of army ants I'd seen on a telly programme once, swarming over the ground and stripping a carcass. I couldn't believe how fast they were. In less than an hour, they'd checked everywhere, taken what they wanted, and put everything else back just as it had been.

Hannah had gone quiet. A stair creaked. Old pipes

hissed in the walls. Then the cold, musty house was still again as if it were waiting too.

Didn't the government people realize Dad was one of them? It was all some huge blunder, had to be.

Shivering, I got under the duvet and stared at the cobwebs and the model warplanes dangling from the ceiling. This had been Dad's room when he was a kid and stayed with his Auntie Hilda. Apparently he'd stayed with her a lot. Dad joked he'd seen more of Hilda than his own parents. He was the kid she'd never had.

I liked seeing Dad's old stuff all mixed up with mine. *One Hundred Riddles and Puzzles*, *Bumper Quiz Book*, *Code-Cracking for Fun*, our big *Bletchley Park* book, and the *Mysteries of the Universe* he'd given me last Christmas and I'd read until the cover dropped off. Hilda had insisted on Dad having his own room and had kept it like a shrine.

Not that I'd known Auntie Hilda much. She'd been in a home for as long as I could remember, Bones the dog always on her lap, a frail old lady who kept asking Dad who he was and if it was teatime yet, until Dad got too sad about the whole thing to take us to visit her any more.

You've got to follow Lily's trail.

I heard Dad's words in my head, remembered the way he'd gripped my arm. But who was Lily?

There was a scratching at my door, and the hinges creaked. I felt a dead weight land on my chest and there was old Bones, snuffling around me with weak little barks. I stroked the ragged patches of fur on his head and he looked at me with his sad, droopy eyes and gave a whining yawn.

My mind flicked over what else Dad had said. Calling me Nathan when he only ever calls me Nat. Swearing at me like that. *Don't ruddy try and hide it like you did the last time.* The way he'd said it, it didn't sound normal. More like he was trying to tell me something, something he didn't want those men to understand, only me.

I remembered Dad's voice, all urgent. *You won't have long,* he'd said, and I had the worrying feeling that I was running out of time, but with no idea what I was supposed to be doing. I guess I felt useless. I guess I wanted to do something, anything, except sit and wait and worry about when Mum would be back and if Dad would be with her, or if the phone would ring any second with news.

So I thought about what Dad had said about homework, but when had I ever hidden homework? I racked my brain and then my heart thumped as a memory came back to me.

It had been a few years ago. We were at Auntie Hilda's house one evening doing one of our monthly visits, to check the house hadn't been broken into and to collect the junk mail from the doormat, that kind of thing. It hadn't been *history* homework, though, I remembered – that was it, it was some poem or other I had to do for English. "Stopping By the Chippie on a Snowy Evening", inspired by Robert Frost. I was in a mood and thought my poem was rubbish and I'd wanted to get rid of it and so I'd shoved it. . .

I scrambled out of bed and snapped on the light. Squinting in the glare, I went over to the writing desk in the corner and started to run my fingers over its wooden front with its carvings of oak trees and flying birds. I was looking for the secret drawer Dad had shown me once. Somewhere there was a fake front and if I could just find the catch. . . There! A wooden panel swung downwards to reveal a small brass handle and I pulled on it in such a hurry that the drawer came right out in my hand. But the drawer was empty. Just like I'd left it when I'd finally retrieved my dire homework poem. What was I expecting to find, anyway?

Annoyed with myself, I tried to get the drawer back in, but it wouldn't go smoothly. I tried to force it closed a few times, then peered inside the narrow space to work out what the problem was, but it was too shadowy to see. I rolled up my sleeves and reached my hand right in, my fingers getting wedged between the cold wooden surfaces, and as I waggled them free, that's when I felt something. My fingertips touched a papery corner that crackled through me like electricity. I eased the edge of whatever it was towards me, worried it would rip. When it had come so far, I got a better grip and slowly slid it out.

I sat on the edge of my bed and looked at the battered brown envelope on my lap. It had something written across the front in looping black ink:

To the Occupiers of Foxglove Cottage.

There was no stamp on it or anything. I peeled the flap open and slid out a single piece of paper going yellow with age, with more spidery handwriting scrawled across it.

Help me,

Look up and through the eye to see where you must go.

Lily Kenley, November 1940

I stared at the paper, breathing hard. Lily again. Lily Kenley. Who *was* she? Her message, it was more than seventy years old. How could it have anything whatsoever to do with Dad? *Follow Lily's trail*, he'd said. I still hadn't got a clue what he was getting at, but was this the start of it, the trail? I sat there, all confused. Excited.

The date was from during the Second World War.

Auntie Hilda liked to collect old stuff from back then – there were piles of nineteen forties things all over the house. Maybe this message had belonged to her. *Look up and through the eye. . .* That sounded like a riddle.

Think literally and laterally. That's what Dad always said to me when we were doing puzzles together. The envelope was addressed to the people in Foxglove Cottage, this house. *Look up?* I looked up at the ceiling, but all I could see were Dad's model warplanes and the dark blue light shade. Up, up, up. . . The most "up" room – that would be the messy attic library, right at the top of the house. Another dumping place for Auntie Hilda's things, and always out of bounds to Hannah and me, though we'd sneaked a look in there a few times. Dad had joked you risked your life just by going through the door: death by falling hatboxes. Mum had said to keep out until she'd had a chance to tidy up. Could going up to the attic library have been what Lily meant?

I refolded the message and put it in my pocket. Not really sure what I was doing, I went out on to the landing, Bones limping after me. I went past the bathroom and Hannah's shut door. The wooden floor was cold through my socks and a clock's ticking echoed eerily up the stairs. I glanced out at the dark drive as I passed the window, but there was no sign of our car. Still not back, but I tried not to think about that. I went to the end of the landing, past the bedroom where Mum and Dad should have been sleeping, to the spiral staircase that led higher up the house, and I started to climb the steep, curving steps. Each one made low screeches under my feet and I was worried I'd wake up Hannah and she'd want to know what I was doing and I wouldn't really know what to tell her. All I knew was that Dad had told me not to say anything to her or Mum. . . But the house stayed silent and I carried on climbing, Bones's claws scratching as he lumbered up after me. I got to the top of the stairs and followed the long, narrow corridor to the attic library.

An icy draught of air came out from under the door on to my feet, and Bones must have felt it on his paws too because he whimpered from behind me. I pressed the handle and peered in at the crammed-together clutter with its splintering tea chests and jumbled furniture and packed bookshelves going high up the wall. The air was thick with the smell of dried-up lavender and damp paper.

There was the skylight caked in grime, and in one corner was the mucky triangular window with its net curtain that looked out towards the back garden. The moon cast silver-grey light across the round, dinted hatboxes and battered leather suitcases and towers of faded newspapers jutting out at every angle. All Auntie Hilda's junk. There was the big clunky bike with a basket on the front, the gramophone on a wonky round table, the battered metal bucket to catch the drips when it rained. Stuff I'd totally forgotten about. The wireless radio in the shape of a box, the oval-shaped tin bath, scattered ration books and records in ripped sleeves. Fusty-smelling clothes hung on nails like floating people, gas masks dangled from the backs of broken chairs, war medals spilt from broken boxes. Auntie Hilda's Second World War museum, though you'd think someone who lived through the war would want to forget about it, like who in their right mind would want to relive all that? Dad said she was nutty, but you could see he was cut up about her getting all forgetful and having to go in an old-people's home.

I felt a dull ache in my chest. When would Dad be back?

The dust tumbled slowly, and cobwebs shivered on the sloping ceiling. Bare water pipes creaked and hissed, and I heard tapping noises in the walls like Morse code messages. Bones gave a bark. I tried the light switch, but it was dead. I made myself go on, but how was I supposed to find anything in here? I'd seen the Special Services people come up, but they must have figured out pretty quickly that nothing had been touched for decades.

I eased past a rickety stepladder and weaved and squeezed slowly through the room. I rounded an old wardrobe and let out a yell. There was someone in the corner, standing in the shadows, looking at me. I saw a lamp and lurched towards it, fumbling to turn it on. Fingers of light spilled out from under its tassels and up the mouldy flower wallpaper with its masses of black and white photographs in frames.

I stood back, panting. It was just the mannequin wearing an RAF uniform. Nutty Auntie Hilda's dressmaking dummy.

I heard a noise outside, like twigs cracking. Mum? In the garden? Not very likely. Scared I'd be seen, I quickly clicked off the lamp and went over to the triangular window and edged back the frayed curtain, rubbing the dirty glass with my fist to see through it. I let out a little gasp. Was that a movement? A figure? I wiped the glass more, smearing dust over the pane. No, I told myself. Just the shadows playing tricks.

And then I saw it.

A perfect oval. About the size of my palm. A thin line scratched on the window, with a smaller circle inside like the staring pupil of an eye.

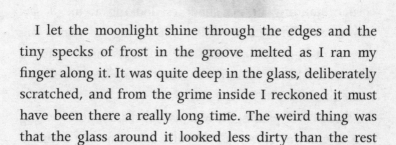

I let the moonlight shine through the edges and the tiny specks of frost in the groove melted as I ran my finger along it. It was quite deep in the glass, deliberately scratched, and from the grime inside I reckoned it must have been there a really long time. The weird thing was that the glass around it looked less dirty than the rest

of the pane, as if it had been wiped over
a hurry. Might Dad have done that, to he
symbol? Might he have known he was going
and quickly made a plan?

Water trickled on to the spongy wood of ⏤ window
ledge from the dripping condensation on the pane. I
looked out at the overgrown garden stretching away
towards Brennan's wood, the tool shed, the hunched-up
air-raid shelter, the old brick well Mum had forbidden
us from going near. I squinted and moved my head to the
side. I craned my neck. The ◎ sign glinted.

Look through the eye to see where you must go.

I hesitated. I bobbed my head, leaned to one side and
back, looking through the sign. My breath caught in my
throat, because when I looked a certain way. . .

There was the sound of a car outside. Headlights swept
the garden. Mum home with Dad? With one last glance at
the window, I tore down the stairs, my mind fizzing like
a firework.

The oval of the eye lined up with the oval of the well.

Not just a bit of a match. Not even a close match.

The edges matched perfectly.

3
The Ghost in the Well

I hurtled downstairs. Was Dad home? I ran into our big sitting room, past the old piano, the chunky oak table, the Welsh dresser with its chipped china plates. Past our stuff still packed in cardboard boxes from the move. Past the walls plastered with Auntie Hilda's war posters and their slogans:

DIG FOR VICTORY; LOOK OUT IN THE BLACKOUT; TELL NOBODY, NOT EVEN HER; KEEP CALM AND CARRY ON.

Past the black metal helmet with a white paint "W", hooked over the fireplace. Past the big dusty glass dome with its stuffed carrier pigeon on a perch inside, its two glass bead eyes staring. I ran into the hallway and flung open the front door.

The dark driveway was empty. The sharp pieces of gravel shone white in the moonlight. But I'd heard an engine. Seen the lights. I was sure there'd been a car!

I shut the door fast and went and stood in the front

room shivering. I couldn't help thinking about the car with tinted windows that had raced away with Dad.

The wind moaned down the chimney, making the last of the wood in the fireplace flare into rusty orange crusts, and the smell of smoke wafted on to me. Bones lumbered past and lay down in his basket whimpering. There was still no noise from Hannah's room. Maybe she'd fallen asleep with her headphones on and hadn't heard my elephant thuds down the stairs.

I stood there in the middle of the front room, trying not to panic, but my hands were trembling and they wouldn't stop. I tried to focus on what I'd seen, the eye on the window matching the shape of the well like that. Was it the next step in Lily's trail, whatever that was, or was I going completely nutty, like old Auntie Hilda? All I knew was that I had to do something else that wasn't waiting and worrying and being too wound up to sleep. . . I made up my mind to check out the well right there and then.

I went back into the hallway, my face brushing against the manky fox fur on the coat stand with its scratchy little paws still attached. I shuddered and zipped my fleece right up to my throat and got my big winter coat from the stand and put on my trainers. I heaved open the top drawer of the hallway cabinet, rifling under a thick address book with a frayed velvety cover that had been there when we moved in, and an old black leather guest book all breaking apart. When would Mum get round to tossing that stuff? I found the bike head torch I'd shoved in there. I still had no idea what I was hoping to do, but I turned the torch on and pulled open the front door.

I made my way along the icy side wall and into the garden. The sky was clear and the moon was almost full, and the tree branches cast weird shadows over me like nets. A loose corner of plastic tied over the woodpile made slapping sounds in the wind, and the long, frozen grass crackled under my feet. I skirted the burnt circle where the bonfire had been, and got to the well with its crumbling brick wall.

Never mess with that well, you hear me? I heard Mum's fussing in my head. *Children drown in wells.* She and Hannah would definitely *not* be happy if they could see me now.

I put the head torch on, leaned over the wall of the well and looked into its gaping hole.

It was a long way down, and I haven't liked heights since – I swallowed and felt my face go sweaty, despite the cold – since that time I fell out of a tree. I tried to force the memory away.

My torch beam stretched along the wet, curving brick walls. I hadn't a clue what I was looking for. I followed the frayed rope to the pool of water, my face reflected there like the trapped ghost in the scary bedtime story Dad used to tell Hannah and me – "The Ghost in the Well".

I heard a noise behind me and spun round. But it was just a magpie that had landed clumsily on the roof of the house and was pecking at the slates. In the distance I heard the dull clang of the church bell striking one.

A flaking rod of metal stuck out from the side of the well, the handle to wind the bucket up, and I clamped my hands on to it and pulled. It wouldn't budge. I pulled harder. Still nothing. It hadn't been wound up for years, I reckoned. It might never turn. Could Dad really have wanted me to be doing this? I banged the cold metal with frustration. What was I even doing messing about out here? I gritted my teeth and wrenched the handle as hard as I could. There was a jolt, then a squealing sound like a small animal dying, and it started to turn. The bucket sloshed up out of the water noisily, dripping black spots.

The handle creaked round and the bucket inched towards me, the muscles in my arms aching with the effort. A thrill rippled through me. But what did I think I'd find? The swinging bucket clattered against the wall of the well and the handle suddenly wouldn't turn any more.

I craned over with the torch. The rope was jammed, stuck between broken bricks part-way down. I leaned over and tugged. My feet left the ground. I tugged again, hard, and the rope came free too suddenly and the bucket swung like a pendulum, losing water and smashing against the side of the well, making me lose my balance. I gave a cry and for a second I was hovering over the lip of the well and scrambling not to tip over into the dark circle of water.

Children drown in wells, a voice whispered in my head, and I seemed to be hanging there for ever, suspended between staying and falling, between the garden alive with moonlight and the echoey dead shadows of the well.

I managed to shift my weight and pivot backwards. I stood there a bit, letting the fear unfurl and sink away, the rope still welded to my numb palms, clouds of condensation tumbling like smoke around me. Then, hand over hand, I carried on pulling, heaving the bucket up. The rope scraped my cold skin painfully and I really wished I'd worn gloves. I gave a final tug and the bucket was out.

I rested it on the wall of the well and looked inside. Water sloshed around in the bottom, and I dipped my fingers in, snapping a skin of ice. Nothing. I turned the bucket over and the water splashed out. Nothing on the base. There was nothing there, just like in the story of the ghost down the well. Nothing but a reflection of my own face and a stupid old battered bucket.

It must have been just one big, weird coincidence I told myself, the sign on the window matching the well like that. Lily's riddle must mean something else. Dad's bound to be home soon anyway, a voice inside me tried to soothe – you can ask him all about it yourself.

I was about to push the bucket back into the well when, just for a second, my torch lit the bottom edge of it and I stopped, not believing what I was seeing at first. I stared along the slimy inside rim of the base, rubbing off the gunk.

To see them you had to angle the bucket a certain way so the scratched letters caught the light.

FIND STRUM. V ◎

You're the best, Nat! I heard Dad say in my head. *A bit tricky, that handle, wasn't it? I knew you'd do it, though. Cracked Lily's code again, didn't you?*

I struggled to think. What did a message from 1940 and a trail by someone called Lily have to do with Dad? I still had no idea, but I reckoned I had possibly just gone and found her next clue.

4

An Open Book

I rubbed my eyes, struggling to wake up.

Dad!

I sat bolt upright, or at least tried to. I was on the settee, still dressed, the sheepskin blanket twisted round me.

It was only just getting dark outside. The little pendulum of the clock on the mantelpiece clicked from side to side and I tried to focus on its luminous Roman numerals. Nearly seven a.m.!

I untangled myself from the blanket and rushed to the window in a total panic that Mum and Dad could have arrived home while I was asleep and that I'd missed them coming in. I pulled back the curtain and rubbed the frost from the inside of the glass. Our car still wasn't back.

I slumped down on the settee, worry like a brick in the bottom of my stomach. For a minute I wondered if I'd dreamt about finding the message on the bucket. Then I saw the head torch on the floor by my damp trainers and I knew it'd been for real.

FIND STRUM. V O

My brain felt too fuzzy to think much about the clue. I felt so cold suddenly. The fire was nearly dead, just bright specks of ash in the grate. I shoved on another log and jabbed it into life with the poker, and little flames danced up along the smoking wood. Behind, flecks of soot glowed red, making face shapes, and the horseshoes nailed to the brickwork glinted in the light.

I stared at the photographs lined up along the mantelpiece, searching for the ones of Dad. There was one of Dad about my age, grinning and holding a model warplane; Dad on a bike too big for him; Dad in the garden with a spade. The clock carried on its ticking like it was counting down to something. I huddled under my blanket and shut my eyes, but all I could see was Dad alone in a room with thick iron bars instead of a door. *Don't be stupid*, I told myself, *he'll be back any time*, but I just couldn't get the image out of my head.

There was the sound of a car outside. At last! I leapt up and I rushed over to the window again. Yes! Mum was back! Dad? I pressed my face right up against the glass so my skin went numb, trying to see.

But only Mum got out.

She stood at the front door as I opened it, her face a grey ghostly colour. She came forward into the hallway and hugged me so it hurt. We stood like that in the cold and then Hannah tramped down the stairs in her pyjamas, the ones with *I am sweet seventeen . . .* in silver sequins on the front and *. . . just so long as I get my lie-in* on the back, her long hair messed up so the red dyed bits stuck out all over.

Mum pulled away from me and shook her head like flies were buzzing around her. She looked exhausted, confused. "They won't let me see him," she said. "I told his solicitor, we've got rights, but Mr Edwards said that the law was changed recently and. . ." She pulled off her hat and unwound her scarf and shook her coat on to the floor. I hung the clothes over the back of a chair as we followed her into the kitchen, and she started opening cupboards and dumping food on the table – a jar of peanut butter, jam, a loaf of bread. Bones looked up at her, his stumpy tail thumping on the floor tiles and his nose twitching.

Mum walked around the kitchen like she was in robot mode, or on auto-pilot, and for some weird reason that thing they tell you on planes came into my head: *those travelling with children, put on your own oxygen mask before helping them with theirs.*

"All I know is," she said, "he's been arrested and he's being held for questioning."

Held for questioning. What did that mean? For some stupid reason I imagined Dad with the *Bumper Quiz Book* from my bedroom in front of him, stooped over a table with a pen and paper, a strict-looking Special Services man standing close by with a stopwatch.

26

"He'll be out by Sunday, though, won't he?" I said, because it was my birthday on Sunday and I'd be thirteen and it was the only thing I could think of to say. But it was a really lame thing to come out with because I shouldn't be thinking about my birthday, I shouldn't even be having a birthday. None of that was important any more, not with Dad *held for questioning*.

"What's the charge, Mum?" Hannah said. "The solicitor must have been told what he's been arrested for, or that's not legal! I just did lessons on police powers at college so I know how it works."

Mum put a raft of way too much bread on the grill pan and lit the gas with a match. "It's what I said. They've arrested him so they can question him. He's not actually been charged with anything yet."

"OK, Mother, I get that! Don't treat us like we're five! Tell us what the *potential* charge is!"

Mum shook out the match and a thick line of smoke poured up from the burnt tip. "Breaking the Official Secrets Act," she said.

I felt my knees tremble under me, like at that moment if I managed to breathe in all the air in the room in one big gulp it still wouldn't be enough. That crazy image crashed back, Dad in the cell with bars on the door.

Hannah gave a snort. "What is this? The nineteen forties?" She chewed at the black polish on her fingernails.

I leaned on the edge of the table. "But he's not done anything wrong," I mumbled.

"*We* know that, love." Mum's words were like raindrops running fast down a window, merging together. "But there's nothing to worry about, OK? We'll have breakfast and then I'll drive back to the solicitor's office so I can try and find out more about what's going on. I've rearranged my shift at the hospital."

"You should get some sleep, Mother!" said Hannah. "You've been up all night, or didn't you realize?"

I wanted so badly to see Dad. I wanted so badly to tell Mum and Hannah about the envelope and the scratched eye and the clue on the bucket.

Mum filled the kettle and put it on to boil.

But Dad had told me to keep it all secret. Was it true what he'd said? Was it really so dangerous to tell Mum or Hannah anything?

I carefully got some china plates from the Welsh dresser, and the butter knives with the ivory handles. I put coffee in the coronation cup Mum liked the best, despite the crack running through King George the Sixth's head.

"We should be able to go and see him!" Hannah scowled. She shoved on a black cardigan and pulled at one sleeve where a thread of wool was unravelling. "Talk about screwed up human rights!"

"How long can they keep him for?" I said.

Hannah frowned. "Without actually charging him? Ninety-six hours."

The kettle screamed, steam pouring from its spout. "Yes, that's what Mr Edwards told me," said Mum, turning off the gas ring. "We're not allowed any contact before then." She got the milk out. *MMXII* spelled the fridge magnets. *MCMXL*. It was a game Dad and I played all the time, making up Roman numerals for each other to work out. We pretty much always wrote in Roman numerals, rather than normal numbers. It drove Mum and Hannah mad.

Looking at the magnets made the clue pop into my head again: *FIND STRUM. V O*, and the *V* straightaway made me think of the number five, but there wasn't a Roman numeral for zero, so it couldn't be that.

"Welcome to democracy!" Hannah splashed milk in her mug and plonked the carton on the table. She slapped at the lukewarm radiator. "When are we getting the heating sorted out? Nothing in this hovel works properly!"

Shut up, Hannah, I thought. Getting annoyed about the house was the last thing we needed right then.

But I was so happy in Auntie Hilda's house as a kid, Dad had said in reply to Hannah's temper about moving, and while he had flowery ideas about his childhood, Mum was thinking mortgage-free, and I was thinking I could get the bus with Josh and Sasha every morning because they both live in the next village. But Hannah was thinking what was wrong with our little terrace in town near her boyfriend Gavin's?

Hannah must have realized how she was behaving because she did shut up and gave Mum a long hug, then knelt and rubbed Bones's head. She might get into moods a lot, but she wasn't that dense.

"I'll come to the solicitor's office with you, Mum," I said.

Mum put spoon after spoon of sugar into her coffee and stirred hard. I eyed the crack in King George's head as I pulled the pan of toast from under the grill, the slices smoking.

"Eat and then go to bed, Mother!" Hannah ordered. "You're no use to anyone knackered." She gave Mum a stern look, then stared out of the window holding her cup, the bright red ends of her long blonde hair nearly dipping in her tea, her unhappy reflection on the rain-speckled pane. Everyone went on about how pretty she was, but all I mostly saw was her in a strop. But right then I guessed exactly what she was thinking, staring out of the window, willing Dad back.

I scraped the burnt parts off a slice of toast with a knife, covering the chipped sink with black bits. I gave a piece to Mum and she nibbled a corner like a distracted mouse.

I traced the cracks across the surface of my plate with a finger, staring at their spider-web-thin lines. "Mum. . ." My throat felt dry as the toast. My voice came out all quiet and sort of broken. "It'll be OK, won't it? When they realize they've made a mistake, I mean, he'll be released. Won't he?"

"Course," said Mum. "A stupid mistake." She stirred her coffee even harder.

"I don't have to go to school today, do I?" I said. There was no way I could face it. "Can I stay here? In case there's news?"

"Up to you, love. Yes, if that's what you want." Mum's face crinkled up in a huge yawn. "I might just have a lie-down after all." She gave us a kiss each and went upstairs.

Hannah and I looked at each other, but I didn't know what to say and then the doorbell rang. Josh. I could tell from the way he pressed the bell, the *Match of the Day* style rhythm, so I told Hannah I'd get it, and then Josh started talking through the letter box like he does when he's nervous, "Friday the eleventh of November, seven fifty-four a.m.," because you always know where you are with dates, he'd told me once. Dates and times. Mum said he probably had a bit of obsessive-compulsive disorder, which she said might be his way of coping with his mum leaving and his dad being a drinker. Whatever the reason, he knew about my dad being taken away. He'd seen how the bonfire party had ended; Mum asking everyone to leave like that; he'd seen the cars of strangers waiting in the lane.

I opened the door and Josh stood there, bag of crisps in hand, the thick, stripy scarf Mum gave him wound round his thin face and ears. His hair stuck up all over like he'd been out for hours, not the fifteen minutes it took him to walk from his house to mine.

He stood in the doorway and then offered me a salt and vinegar crisp. We stood there crunching.

Then the next minute Sasha was standing there too with her perfect black hair in a rainbow bobble hat and her black puffer jacket and her woolly pink mittens, all full of questions. "Is your dad back, Nathan? What's going on?"

I told them the story, as much as Mum had told me. All except the breaking the Official Secrets Act part. I couldn't bring myself to tell them about that.

"They won't say why they're arresting him? Oh God, Nathan." Sasha wrapped her arms around me so I could smell this vanilla kind of smell in her hair, which made my eyes start to sting, so I said I had to help my mum with something and I wasn't going to school.

"Not going to school?" repeated Josh, like the very idea went against all Einstein's theories. "But it's Friday. We're watching that film in the hall. Then there's the footie match, us versus the teachers," he added, like it was the Battle of Britain or something.

"Do you think Nathan cares about all *that*?" Sasha tutted at him. "Look, we've got to go, Nathan, or we'll miss the bus." She gave me another hug. ". . .But we'll be round straight after school – *straight after*!"

I said OK and closed the door.

"Text you soon," called Sasha through the letter box. Then they were gone.

I stood there with my back against the door awhile, not able to move. I *did* care. I wished I *could* go into school with them and watch the film, and play football against the teachers as if nothing had happened. But everything was different now. I felt it pressing down on me – Dad's arrest; the weight of my secret promises to him. *Follow Lily's trail. Don't tell anyone.*

CARELESS TALK COSTS LIVES Auntie Hilda's Second World War poster shouted at me from the wall opposite.

I went into the front room. Hannah was dressed in tight black jeans and a leather jacket and boots up to her knees, and her eyes were all done up in black, and she dumped a tray down on the coffee table. A mug of hot chocolate, toast smeared in butter and without any burnt bits, an egg in an egg cup and a cellar of salt. "Eat that," she ordered. "I'm going out for a bit. On the bus. To see Gavin. I'll be back soon. You'll be all right? If Mum wakes up and she needs anything or she wants me to look after you or there's any news, you tell her to ring me straightaway, OK?"

I tried to smile. "Thanks. But I don't need a babysitter."

"I know, baby brother." She gave me a punch on the arm and tried to smile back. She opened her mouth to say something more, then closed it again. She nodded and left.

I cracked the egg on the table and heaped the pieces of shell at the edge of my plate. The yolk burnt my mouth, but I suddenly realized how hungry I was and finished the lot. I sat and sipped my hot chocolate. Hannah had put loads of sugar in, just the way Dad made it.

I had to help Dad! Not mope about feeling sorry for myself. My mind went to the message on the bottom of the bucket again. Some woman called Lily Kenley had made a trail. "But why?" I said out loud. Why go to all that trouble? What had her trail got to do with my dad, anyway? What was at the end? An *X marks the spot* and a

33

chest of treasure? An explanation? That would be enough. The truth about what was going on.

FIND STRUM. V O

My mind whirred. *Think literally and laterally.* Concentrate, I told myself. You worked out the last ones, you can do the same with this. That *STRUM* thing – the word seemed familiar somehow. I was sure I'd heard it before.

"Strum," I said to Bones. "Strum. Strum. Strum." He woofed and licked my buttery fingers.

Dad's voice flashed into my head. *Choose a book, Nat. Choose a Strum book, one to ten.* I was on my feet. That's what Dad had called them, wasn't it?

I went quietly back upstairs, my brain racing the whole way. Mum's bedroom door was slightly open and I saw her sleeping inside. I tiptoed past and climbed the spiral staircase towards the attic library again.

"Dad read them to us when we were younger, Bones!" I whispered to him as he shuffled up the steps after me. "He called them the Strum books and I'm sure they were kept up here."

I got into the attic and managed to switch the lamp on and stood gazing at the shelves and shelves of old books. There were hundreds of the things, thousands maybe. More books here, probably, than in the entire village library before the council closed it down. The whole of one wall was covered in them, right to the ceiling, with a dodgy-looking stepladder at one end and the RAF mannequin looking serious at the other like he was on guard duty.

"How am I supposed to find them in that lot?"

Bones looked at me mournfully and sneezed. I couldn't even remember the colour of the Strum books, it was that many years since I'd seen one. It had been back during the time of our monthly visits to check on Auntie Hilda's house. Some rainy Saturday or other when Hannah and I couldn't play in the garden, and Dad read to us instead.

"Where first, Bones? Left or right?"

Bones yawned and lay down on his side on the tatty rug.

"Left it is, then." I clicked on the lamp and started to search, bending double to see the very bottom shelf, one book at a time, my eyes picking out the titles on the spines in the dimly lit row. "Worth lots of doggy treats, they are," I called quietly to Bones and he licked his mouth with a big pink tongue.

Dad had always said the Strum books were valuable and that we should treat them really carefully. . . Maybe he'd already known about Lily's trail back then; maybe that's why he was so fussy about the Strum books. Then why had he never told me anything about it until now? I couldn't help feeling hurt at the idea of Dad keeping secrets from me.

A spider dropped towards us on its thread like it was trying to listen in. Cloud shadows scuttled over the floor from the skylight. Sleet splattered the glass. I eyed the stepladder and hoped I'd find the books on the lower shelves. Heights weren't my strong point.

A triangle of weak sunlight jutted like an arrow from the net curtain as I continued searching. No luck on the bottom row. Next shelf up then.

By row five I was on tiptoes. It was taking ages and I had a crick in my neck from stretching. In the distance I heard the church bells and my fingers seemed to flick along the books in time with their clangs. Eleven o'clock already? There was a faint boom, like a cannon firing. For Remembrance Day, I realized. Today was the eleventh of November and they'd be having a service in town, and then a bigger one on Sunday. At school, Sasha and Josh would be doing a two-minute silence for people who had died in the war.

I carried on my search, and I was near the end of the fifth shelf when Bones started pawing at me and weaving through my legs and I lost my balance and grabbed at books to try and stop myself going down, but they came out of the shelves and started falling and I ended up on my back as books clattered down all around me.

Bones sat on my chest and licked my face. His tail banged the floor, sending up swirls of dust. "It's not lunchtime yet!" I said, pushing him off and getting to my feet. I started picking up the spilled books and shoving them back, but as I did I saw there was another book tucked behind, pressed flat against the wall.

I tugged it out. A fat notebook with an old smell and

a mottled grey front. I flicked to the first page. There was something written on the inside cover, and as I read it I stumbled backwards into a pile of newspapers.

Lily Kenley, born 21.03.1902

"Lily!" I hissed to Bones, and he gave a confused yelp.

Lily again. There was something else written below her name. The handwriting was hard to read because the letters were all scratchy and blotchy like they'd been done too fast.

I have to save my dad. If only. . .

I brought the book closer to make out the letters.

If only I can break the code.

Weird. What was that about? What did this Lily person have to save her dad from? I wondered. Then there were pages and pages of letters in pencil on the faintly lined paper. Close-spaced lines of writing. Only not words. There were all these groups of three capital letters: ~~BBC~~ ~~BBD~~ ~~BBE~~. . . Lists and lists of them, each crossed out with a neat single line, going on for pages and pages.

I wondered if Dad knew about this notebook. I'd found it pretty much by fluke and I'd no idea what any of it meant, or whether it was part of the trail, but it was Lily's, so it could be important, right? I pushed the notepad to where I'd find it again and carried on scanning along the shelf for the Strum books.

I fumbled with the stepladder and went up a couple of rungs, my head on a level with the sixth shelf up. I stared along the crammed-in book spines, then got down and shifted the ladder along and climbed up again.

I stopped. There was a group of little books with the same kind of dark blue spine with gold bands, and when I counted quickly, there were . . . ten! I pulled the first one out and read the flaky gold lettering on the cover.

Stories To Read Under Moonlight

My mouth broke into a giant-sized grin. *Stories To Read Under Moonlight. STRUM.* I'd *known* they were here somewhere!

Volume I: Treasure Island. The first book of the set. I pulled out the others and made a pile of them on the floor. Volume II: Robinson Crusoe; Volume III: Sherlock Holmes; Volume IV: The Secret Garden. . . But which of the ten books was I supposed to be looking in? *STRUM. V O. . .*

Volume V: Fantastical Fairy Tales.

V. Volume five. Was that it?

I went over to the lamp and thumbed slowly through the pages and their detailed colour drawings. There were hideous trolls under bridges and witches on broomsticks and goblins with sharp fingernails and giants swiping spiked clubs. There was the "Ghost in the Well" story Dad had read to Hannah and me. I got to the last page. THE END. So what now?

STRUM. V O

I tried to think of all the things an O shape could be. It might be a letter or a zero. I thought about the circle of the well and the round, battered bucket. Maybe it was a symbol for something in a picture.

"Is it *this*?" I used a thumb and finger to make a circle round my eye like I was watching Bones through a keyhole, and he woofed a bit at me. "This?" I curled myself into a round shape on the dusty rug, hugging my knees and he gave a little whine. "This, maybe?" My mouth made a round, scared shape at him and he barked in a disturbed sort of way and went to sit under the gramophone table.

I leafed through the book again, and when I looked closer, I noticed that each picture had an extra tiny part to the caption. *Plate A*, said the first. *Plate B*, the second – something to do with the way it was printed in the olden days, maybe. I flicked forward fast, my fingers tingling. If the V meant volume five, might the O be the letter of a picture? *Plate D*, *Plate F*, *Plate J, K, L*. . . I quickly turned the pages and at last there it was. Plate O.

They followed the breadcrumbs
trail, but found themselves at the end.

There was a drawing of a scared-looking Hansel and

Gretel in the woods, bent to the ground while birds circled overhead.

I was excited, but confused too. Worry nagged at me. Had I found the next clue? Was it just a picture and a caption? How was I supposed to work that out?

Bones whined and stared at me, licking his muzzle. "In a minute, greedy," I told him. "I'm thinking."

"Nathan?" I heard Mum's tired voice calling. I quickly hid the Strum book in my pocket and went back downstairs, Bones clambering behind me.

TELL NOBODY, NOT EVEN HER, the poster blared at me from the wall as I went into the front room to find her. Mum stood there bleary-eyed and still in her dressing gown, her face all pinched up. She peered at the clock on the mantelpiece. "God, how did it get to nearly lunchtime already? Are you OK, love?"

"Fine," I said, as casually as I could. Lying to Mum, all these secrets – I felt myself squirm.

"Have there been any phone calls?" she asked.

"No."

Mum looked grim and snatched up the phone handset. "Then I'm ringing Mr Edwards right now to find out what's going on!" She went into the kitchen and I heard her talking to Dad's solicitor – loud and getting louder. "But when will they tell us *exactly* what he's supposed to have done?" Pause. "I know the law's been toughened, but this waiting is hell!" Pause. "Well, as soon as you know anything, Sam, *please*. . ."

"No fresh news," said Mum, coming back into the front room. She thumped a couple of cushions straight and tossed them back on the settee.

There were noises at the front door and Hannah walked in. "Dad?" she asked straightaway.

"No fresh news," said Mum again like she was a recording. "They're still questioning him." She moved over to Hannah and stroked her hair.

Hannah looked at me, then looked away. "I've got a journalism assignment to do for college," she mumbled, and went upstairs.

Mum wandered into the kitchen and I heard her yank open the door of the freezer. "Mr Edwards said he wants to have a meeting with us this afternoon," she called. "At his office on Fitzroy Street."

A meeting with the solicitor? It sounded a bit heavy. I tried to push away my panic and focus on the clue. I got the Strum book out of my pocket and stared hard at Plate O. *They followed the breadcrumbs trail, but found themselves at the end*.

There was the sound of rummaging and tinkling ice from the kitchen, and then Mum asking me what I fancied for lunch, but I hardly heard her. An idea started forming in my head. I went over to the framed map on the wall by the Welsh dresser. It was a faded black ink thing, dated eighteen hundred and something, a map of the area. . .

"Spag bol or fish pie?" Mum was calling.

. . .There was *Foxglove Cottage* and *Brennan's Wood*

behind it. There was the winding track through the trees, the one that started at the end of Auntie Hilda's garden. . .

"*Nathan!*"

"Er . . . fish pie. No, spaghetti!" I peered at the label written along the path. . .

. . . THE BREADCRUMBS TRAIL.

I tapped the words with delight so the map went all wonky.

I couldn't help laughing to myself. *The Breadcrumbs Trail!* I should have remembered it before! That's what Dad said Auntie Hilda called the path through Brennan's Wood we went on. Only people who'd lived round here for years would know; there was no signpost or anything. It couldn't just be a coincidence. I had to be on to something!

I traced the path with my finger. *TRAIL'S END* it said where the line met the road. Lily's next clue had to be along that path! Now all I had to do was go out and. . .

Mum came in and I quickly shoved the Strum book behind a cushion. "It's in the microwave," she said. "Won't be long."

"I need to go out," I said.

Mum glanced at her watch. "Where to?"

"Just a walk," I said. I hated lying to her, but I was dying to get on the Breadcrumbs Trail and find the next clue.

"We've to set off for the solicitor's at half one, so I want you to eat now, thank you. There's snow forecast for this afternoon," she said, like if I didn't get some food inside

42

me before then I was doomed. "Who ever heard of snow in early November?" she mumbled.

I sidled towards the door, pulling on my coat, slipping the little Strum book from under the cushion into my pocket. "I'm not so hungry yet. I had a big breakfast and. . ."

"You're eating first!" Mum said in her *absolutely no arguments* voice, like as long as she kept us stuffed with food, everything would be all right.

I stomped into the kitchen and watched the plastic tray turn inside the microwave. Round and round it went. Thoughts spun in my head. The words Lily had scribbled in her notebook. *I have to save my dad. If only I can break the code.* What did that mean? Round and round and round. . .

The microwave beeped, making me jump. I took the tray out and peeled off the plastic lid, roasting my fingers on the steam. I slapped the whole thing on a plate. I jabbed a fork into the runny sauce, stabbing out strands of spaghetti and eating as fast as I could without burning my mouth; then, hearing Mum go upstairs, I shovelled the rest into Bones's bowl before he drooled himself to death and he chomped it down in ten seconds flat, splattering bits of mince and red blobs all over.

I opened the back door as quietly as I could, breathing in the cold, damp air. The light was murky, as if it was going dark already. Mist reached across the garden, and the grass was spiky with frost. The well crouched on the overgrown lawn, and trees huddled at the far end where the woods began, like they were sharing secrets. I zipped up my coat and went quickly past the tool shed, past the well, past the air-raid shelter, heading for the gap in the hedge with its half-rotted wooden gate, the gate I'd been through loads of times with Dad. What was I going to find? What *could* there be that I wouldn't have noticed before? Whatever it was, I had to be there and back before we needed to go to the solicitor's, so I had to get moving.

I checked my watch, then started out along the Breadcrumbs Trail.

5

The Breadcrumbs Trail

At first the path followed a little brook that was all choked up with brambles, before twisting deeper into the trees. I heard the church bell clang over and over and I checked my watch. Twelve noon. I passed the blackberry patch where we'd stuff our faces in the late summer, and the spot where Dad and I would lie and watch clouds make shapes through the trees. But now it was misty and cold and unwelcoming. Damp, rotting leaves made the path slippery, and feathery nettles stung my ankles.

What was I looking for? Something that would get Dad off? A gingerbread house and a witch to put me in the oven? From somewhere behind me, a twig cracked. I spun around, seeing nothing through the thickening mist. I hurried on, stepping over fallen trunks covered in slimy moss. I just had to hope I'd know whatever it was I was looking for when I saw it, something I'd missed all the previous times I'd been here. On I went, walking slowly to check each side of the path for anything that might be something.

I'd been walking a while and found nothing. I stopped at the big oak we called the Robin Hood tree. Not my favourite place. I glanced up nervously at the frayed piece of rope that used to be a rope swing, remembering that day and how I couldn't stand heights since then.

It happened when I was about six. Dad had somehow managed to get the rope looped round a high branch, with a thick, short bit of wood for a seat. We came to play here all the time, me and Hannah and Dad. I remembered being on the swing, making monkey noises as I swept from side to side; Hannah was in stitches. Then the weird cracking, ripping sound that seemed to go on for ever and then the falling, the falling and the landing with a scream, my right arm twisted under me. Then Dad running and running; carrying me back to the house, with tears streaming down his face. I got a broken arm, but it could have been a broken neck, and I've hated heights ever since. I don't think Dad ever forgave himself.

The wind got stronger, making the bare branches shiver, and dark clouds were building up in the sky. I zipped my jacket tighter around my neck and walked on fast. The mist made my face damp and I shoved my hands in my pockets to keep them warm. Why had Lily Kenley made a trail at all? If Dad knew about it, why had he waited until now to tell me? How could an old trail like

46

this be important anyway?

Mum and Hannah could help me understand it, I thought. But Dad had been clear. *The more people who know, the more dangerous it is.* I felt my palms go all clammy. Dad must know there was no choice about keeping the trail secret. No matter what, I trusted him. I'd always trust my dad.

I trudged forward. I'd be at the road soon, the official end of the Breadcrumbs Trail, and I still hadn't found a thing.

The path wound on. The ground went up to a kind of hill smothered in rhododendron bushes, and then there was a big dip on the other side, a sloping basin of mud covered in patches of tangled ferns.

Another twig snapped behind me. Birds flashed between the branches overhead like little missiles. A magpie cawed my name from a tree. It was just my imagination, right, like the phantom car on our drive last night, and the figure half-glimpsed in the garden?

A last muddy climb and I'd be at the edge of the road. I looked at my watch – it was after half past one! Panicking, I got out my mobile. Mum should have phoned me if I was late. Why hadn't she?

SEARCHING said the screen in ghostly green.

Stupid! I'd forgotten the signal could be dodgy in the woods. She might have been trying to get hold of me! I *so* had to get home.

I looked at the phone screen again. *Still searching,* I

thought grimly, just like me. No sign of any next clue. I'd have to go back over the trail again later and hope I found something then.

I sprinted up the slope to the road. It'd be quicker to go back that way now. I stood on the edge of the frosty tarmac and was about to step on to it when I heard a car coming. Maybe it was getting spooked in the woods that had made me all jumpy, but I swerved back to hide just in time. A car revved past. Our car. Mum and Hannah in it. I was in *big* trouble now.

I snapped open my phone. Out of the hollow, I had a signal again.

FOUR MISSED CALLS shouted the screen.

Mum *had* been trying to phone me. She was probably going mental.

Stupid. Stupid. I stared after the red tail lights, then clambered up to the road as I started to phone her back. But my foot caught on something and nearly sent me sprawling on to the grassy verge. I crouched to look why I'd tripped.

It was a rectangle of rock, and the weird thing was it looked like the thick tufts of grass and weeds and the leaves around it had been cleared a bit, and there was a thin border of bare soil as if someone had recently tried to dig it out.

I felt a rush of excitement. Might Dad have done that? I remembered how the window in the attic room had been wiped clean. For me?

"They followed the breadcrumbs trail." I quickly muttered the caption from the Strum book to myself. "But found themselves at the end."

They found themselves at the end! I thought back to the old map, with TRAIL'S END written where the path met the road. Right here. X marks the spot!

My breath came out in grey-white bursts as I scraped at the surface of the stone. It was all crusted up with lichens and they were hard to make out but I saw now that there were letters on it, words! I ran my fingers in their worn grooves.

BLETCHLEY PARK
6 MILES

I'd found an old milestone, fallen over on its side so it laid flat on the ground. It must have been half-buried before, covered over with soil and plants.

Might Dad have made the stone easier to find? Could it have been his way of helping me follow the trail?

A scrap of sunlight lit the milestone. *Bletchley Park*! Did that mean I should go there next? I'd been there on a school trip once with Sasha and Josh. It was where they'd worked out secret messages during the Second World War. Bletchley Park, that code-cracking place.

I remembered Lily's words from her notebook – *If only I can break the code* – was there a link? I scoured the milestone and my eye caught more lettering. I peered

close, using my fingernails to pick off the brittle patches
of lichens.

LI. . .

They were smaller letters, still old-looking, but more
messy than the others. I imagined the milestone when it
had been standing up straight. These extra letters weren't
on the front, but on a hidden place along one edge.
Grooves scratched deep like graffiti or something.

I heard a bus crunching its gears not far away. I checked
my watch, thinking fast. It was too late to call Mum to
come back for me now. The bus would take me into town.
I definitely had to be on that one so I could get to the
solicitor's. I ran my mind back through what Mum had
told me – *Mr Edwards, Fitzroy Street.*

There were at least fifty metres to the stop, and I could
hear the bus getting closer, but I stayed bent over the
milestone, prising off clods of soil to uncover the other
letters. . .

LION EAGLE

I ran my fingers over the words, breathing fast. If I'd
had doubts before, I knew now for sure. Lily's trail was
real, important. Dad wanted me to follow it. He believed
in me, believed that I really could do it. It might not make
any sense now, but give me time and. . .

Just then my mobile beeped. I fumbled to get it out of my pocket and set off at a sprint as the bus came into view.

At solicitor's with hannah.

The screen juddered as I ran.

Where r u? Go round to
josh's and get his dad to
drive you here asap. Mum.

My heart thudded. It must be something serious, trusting me in a car with Josh's dad behind the wheel, even if he says he never drinks and drives any more. There must be news about Dad. It might be good news, I tried to tell myself, but for some reason only horrible thoughts spiralled round my head.

A drop of icy rain splashed the display as I shoved the mobile back in my pocket and flung out my arm for the bus.

6
Mr Edwards

"Where the heck have you been?" said Mum, shooting up from her chair in the waiting room as I crashed through the door of the solicitor's, slipping to a stop on the lino floor in my wet trainers. "It's after two thirty in the afternoon!"

Except she didn't say heck.

Hannah caught my arm and pulled me to the side. "Remember *mo-biles*?" she said sarcastically. "You know? That wonderful invention of modern times?"

I peeled down my drenched rain hood. "Did something happen?" I croaked.

"Where *were* you?" Mum gave me a suspicious look. "I kept calling."

"Sorry," I mumbled. "I. . ."

"Mr Edwards will see you now."

Saved by the secretary. A woman in a long blue dress led us through a grey door and down a long corridor to a lift and up to the top floor and through another grey door with a brass plate that said:

MR SAMUEL EDWARDS

A man wearing glasses and a black suit came out and shook our hands, half his mouth turned up in a smile. "Please," he said. "Come into my office. Tea all round, please, Susan." The secretary nodded and left.

Mr Edwards faced us across a big desk and linked his fingers together like he was praying over the stuff on it. A laptop, a neat pile of documents, a telephone, a desk lamp, a box of paper hankies, a Union Jack paperweight, a posh gold pen in a holder. There was a framed photo of a boy smiling over the candles of a birthday cake, another of an older girl on a pony.

"Thanks for coming," he said very slowly. He took off his glasses and rubbed them with a white handkerchief like he was waving a surrender. "You must all be very anxious, so I'll tell you as much as I'm able to at this point in time."

The secretary came in with a tray, and Mr Edwards paused again while the cups were handed out, and he motioned to the silver pot of sugar cubes, like we all had to have one before he could go on. Mum splashed in three lumps and stirred her tea hard. Hannah grabbed one and crunched it between her teeth.

"I think you know by now that Leon is being

questioned over some really rather serious allegations," Mr Edwards said in that slow voice of his, like words cost a lot, which they probably did, and he wanted us to get our money's worth saying them.

"We know," said Hannah. "Breaking the Official Secrets Act."

Mr Edwards gave a small, sad smile. "I'm afraid the charges have been stepped up."

Mum gave him a sideways stare. "What do you mean *stepped up*?"

Mr Edwards shifted in his seat and fingered his paperweight. "Leon is now being questioned under the Prevention of Terrorism Act."

Hannah gasped. Mr Edwards's words hung in the room like thick drops of glue sticking the air together. *Prevention of Terrorism.* I felt my fingernails digging into my palms. My dad was no terrorist!

"'*Section 58: Collection of information useful for a terrorism act*'," Mr Edwards read from a paper on his desk. "'*Section 59: Inciting terrorism overseas*'. The pre-charge detention can be up to twenty-eight days with a special warrant. At the moment, the situation's stable," he continued quickly. "Leon hasn't actually been charged with anything yet, and until he is. . ." He ran a finger where his shirt collar rubbed his neck. "I'm monitoring your dad's case carefully, believe me, and making sure he gets the full legal protection he's entitled to."

Stable. I imagined Dad balanced on a tightrope between tall buildings.

Mum's cup clattered down in her saucer and she let out a strained laugh.

"I understand your distress, Mrs Vane. I was as shocked as you were when I found out Leon had been arrested, believe me. You know that we were friends at school together. But he had classified files on his computer at work and. . ."

"Course he did!" cut in Mum. "He works at the Ministry of Defence, for goodness' sake!"

"They were files he didn't have clearance for."

Mum went quiet. That was serious, then.

"He's being questioned about stealing confidential military files and selling them overseas."

Mum stayed very quiet. That was really serious.

Mr Edwards wiped some sweat off his forehead.

"I don't need to tell you the implications," he said quietly. "With our country involved in several armed conflicts at the present time. . ."

"When do we get to see my dad?" cut in Hannah. "We have rights."

Mr Edwards sighed and shifted the position of some papers on his desk. "I was telling your mum earlier, given a few recent events I'm sure you know about, there's been some rapid tightening of the anti-terrorism laws. The family are allowed no contact while a suspect is being held. Not before he's formally charged, and even then. . ."

"*What?*" Mum said, her voice straining.

"No contact at *all*?" I couldn't help blurting.

Mr Edwards looked at me and tapped his fingers on his desk. He tried to smile, which made his face wrinkle up like a Guy Fawkes mask. "Your mother tells me it's your birthday on Sunday, Nathan. Maybe I can arrange a call between you and your dad, on compassionate grounds?" He fiddled with the cuff of his jacket, looking shifty. "No promises, though."

"What if he's found guilty?" Mum fiddled with her wedding ring, her face flushed, like she was embarrassed even thinking that.

Mr Edwards leaned forward, the way I'd seen Mum comfort relatives at the hospital. "We're looking at a long prison sentence, Mrs Vane."

I just sat there, like I was tied to the chair.

"How long?" asked Mum, her voice all scratchy like an old record.

Mr Edwards joined his hands together and pressed two fingers over his lips. "Perhaps life."

Mum gave a little cry. "Bit extreme, isn't it?" she said, her voice strangely faint.

Hannah kept tugging and tugging at her hair.

"The leaked information. . ." Mr Edwards was choosing his words carefully. "It is already thought to have led to fatalities in the military."

Hannah knocked over her tea, soaking the papers on the desk, and Mr Edwards rushed to pick them up. "What?"

she said shakily. "Soldiers *died* because of it?"

"Information about their positions fell into enemy hands," said Mr Edwards. "That's all I can say about it at the present time."

Soldiers died. Life in prison. The words like a bomb falling. Then the explosion that changes everything. But you can't move. You're trapped under rubble and it's pressing at your chest and you know nothing can ever be the same again but you just can't move.

Life in prison.

Memories of Dad flickered in my mind like a film reel. Dad and me writing our names with sparklers on Bonfire Night, Dad and me playing football on the fields, Dad and me singing songs in the car on hot summer holidays, Dad running alongside my bike as I wobbled along, Dad reading me a book as I sipped hot chocolate. Dad meeting me at the school gate and lifting me on his shoulders so I was taller than anyone. . . Dad carrying me in his arms after I fell from that tree.

I just wanted him back. I just wanted my dad back.

I felt a hand on my shoulder, and then Mr Edwards pulled a fist of paper tissues from the box and dabbed spilled tea off his table. He smiled at us, that lopsided smile of his, but I saw the worry on his face and I saw it wasn't fake.

Dad had said not to trust anyone, but why not Mr Edwards – he'd help me surely? I felt the weight of my secret again, like a chunk of stone inside me.

Mum stayed sitting there, her mouth sagging open.

"Well, they've obviously got the wrong person," Hannah said. "So how are you going to get him off?"

"The odds are not looking good at the moment, I'm afraid," Mr Edwards said. "Planning for if he *is* charged, we *do* need to discuss his best defence case, but it's not simple." He paused to throw the tissues in the bin under his desk and I saw a bald spot on the top of his head. "The case against him – frankly, it's stronger by the hour. The prosecution have got footage of Leon going into the Ministry of Defence offices after hours. There's also footage of him at secret meetings, allegedly receiving money in exchange for military secrets."

"*What*?" Mum gaped.

Mr Edwards leaned forward a little. "The best defence case we have is this." He paused to clear his throat. "Leon mentioned to me that he was collecting evidence on corrupt members of staff."

I stared at the solicitor. What was he saying?

"He says it was true he was at some of these meetings," Mr Edwards went on, "but he was acting under cover."

"What, like he was James Bond or someone?" spluttered Mum. "Would the judge take that claim seriously, do you think?"

"More than likely the prosecution would see this as a weak attempt to blame others for his crimes. He refuses to say anything about it to the authorities, which doesn't put him in a good light. I understand Special Services removed everything from the house?"

Mum nodded like a dashboard toy. "All Leon's stuff, yes. His papers and his computer data, everything from his study."

Mr Edwards nodded back, slowly. "I'm just waiting for copies to see if anything can help Leon's case. But the prosecution's arguments *are* becoming very persuasive."

For a moment he seemed distracted, staring at the family photos on his desk. "They find your weak spots," he muttered. "Apply pressure." I saw his hands were tight balls and his fingers had gone white at the tips, and I don't know why but he had this kind of scrunched, haunted look. It didn't look right.

Mr Edwards cleared his throat. "What we really need to do is find the evidence Leon collected."

I blinked hard.

"If we find the evidence – if this evidence actually exists – it could prove his innocence."

I sat there staring at my hands, willing my face not to go death white or bright red and give me away. I remembered Dad by the bonfire, the way he'd held my arm. *You've got to follow Lily's trail, Nat. Without evidence we've got nothing. . . I found something out. . .*

It hit me then. Where all these clues were leading. I hardly dared to think about it. The evidence, whatever it was, could *that* be at the end of Lily's trail? The evidence needed to get Dad off!

"This evidence. . ." Hannah twisted the dyed ends of her hair. "Aren't there any other copies? Dad was bound to have done backups! Why doesn't he just tell the Special Services where it is so they'll release him?" She narrowed her eyes at Mr Edwards. "Why doesn't he tell *you*?"

"Yes, can't you just ask *Leon*?" said Mum, all in a fluster.

Mr Edwards pulled the lid off his gold pen, and then clicked it back on, then pulled it off again. "Leon still hasn't told me its whereabouts."

"Why not?" snapped Mum.

"No doubt he has his reasons," said Mr Edwards, and I couldn't be sure, but he seemed to have that scrunched-up look again, and I saw him glance at the photos on his desk, but he carried on quickly. "If he is charged and I'm going to make any kind of convincing argument, I really need to see this evidence before the prosecution does so I can act on it. I can help, but unless the evidence is found, we're looking at a very flimsy case." Mr Edwards shook his head. "Have you *no* ideas where Leon might have hidden it?"

Mum shook her head back, like she was still playing a copying game, and Hannah gave a shaky shrug.

"Nathan?" His eyes seemed to burrow into me.

I kept looking at my hands, which Dad told me is a sure sign of a liar. I forced myself to put my head up and look him straight in the face. "No," I said, feeling my face go all hot. "No idea."

Mum sat up. "What exactly is this evidence supposed to show?"

"I'm afraid I don't really know yet, Mrs Vane."

I could see Mum fuming at that, getting in a real flap. "Well if *you* don't, who *does*?"

"Hannah, is there anything you want to tell me?" Mr Edwards avoided Mum's glare. "Any extra information that might help your dad?"

Hannah shook her head. "Whatever it is, he didn't do it," she said.

My stomach turned over. Was this the point I was supposed to tell him about Lily's trail? All I could see in my head was Dad lit by the bonfire saying *Don't trust anyone, Nat*, but this Mr Edwards, he was different, surely. He was Dad's solicitor. They'd been friends at school together and everything. I took a swig of tea, my secret pressing on my ribcage. I had to tell them, surely. I wanted to. *Tell them!* a voice inside me hissed. *Before it's too late!*

Don't, another voice came. *It's too dangerous. Don't trust anyone.* I straightened up. Dad hadn't told Mr Edwards where the evidence was, had he? There had to be a reason. If the evidence was hidden at the end of Lily's trail, Dad wanted *me* to find it.

"Nathan." Mum turned to me. "*You* were the last one to talk to your dad. Did he say anything about evidence?"

I saw Mr Edwards looking at me intently over his cup, and then – it was really fast so no one else saw – I'm sure he pressed a finger to his lips. *Keep quiet. Don't say a word.*

I tried to keep my voice from shaking. "No, Mum," I said. "Nothing."

"Mrs Vane." Mr Edwards pressed a button on his phone and stood up. "If you'd go with Susan into the next room for a few minutes, there're some papers we need you to sign urgently – personal information permissions, that kind of thing." Mum opened her mouth to speak, but he just ploughed on. "Perhaps, Hannah, you'd like to give your mum some moral support." He gave a sympathetic laugh. "There're quite a few pages to get through."

Mum gave a short nod. "We'll be back soon, Nathan. You stay put."

The Susan woman came in and herded Mum and Hannah out.

As soon as the door clicked shut, Mr Edwards leaned across the desk, talking really fast, proving he could speed up his speech when he wanted to. "It's rather irregular of me, without your mum present, Nathan, and we haven't got long, but extreme cases need extreme measures. We have to find that evidence. It's absolutely vital. Is there anything else your dad told you before he was arrested?"

I looked at Mr Edwards, at the way his face creased in a frown like he really cared, the pictures of his kids on the desk in front of him. I thought about the secret sign he'd made to me, helping me to keep quiet in front of Mum and Hannah. Maybe I could trust him after all. He and Dad had been friends at school together, like me and Sasha and Josh were. It would be such a relief to tell someone about the trail. He might help us with Lily's next clue. He might know what *lion eagle* meant and when we found the evidence he could. . . I opened my mouth to speak.

"No?" Mr Edwards butted in loudly before I could reply. "Well, if you *do* think of anything, or find anything, I'll give you my business card so you can contact me."

We heard voices in the corridor. Mum and Hannah coming back. Mr Edwards wrote something across it at the speed of light with his posh gold pen and pressed the card into my hand. I read it and I stared at him, but he shot me a fierce look and there was no doubt what he was telling me this time – he pressed a finger firmly to his lips.

THIS OFFICE IS BUGGED
YOUR HOUSE WILL BE TOO

"My direct line is there," he said loudly. I saw he'd crossed out his usual mobile number and written another over it. "So if you *do* think of anything."

The door swung open and he lifted the lid of his laptop. I sat there staring at him like an idiot, but he didn't look up from the screen again. "Just another brief word, Mrs Vane, Hannah," he called as they came back in. "Nathan, wait outside, could you?"

The grey door closed shut behind me. I went over to the window in the corridor, pushing my nose against the glass, trying to take in what had just happened. Our house *bugged*? The Special Services people could easily have done that during their search. I tried to think back over all my conversations, fretting. Had I given anything away?

The rain had turned to snow. Little flakes stuck on the pane. Too cold for November.

Whose side was Mr Edwards on? Why *hadn't* Dad told him where the evidence was? For that matter, why *didn't* he just tell the Special Services people straight if it would get him off? None of it made any sense. Dad didn't trust any of them, was that it? On the other hand, Mr Edwards had warned me; given me a private number to ring him on. It was too confusing.

This evidence – what could it be? What would it say about Dad? Would it really get him off, or might it get him into even more trouble?

The town spread out below me, like the view from a plane. Lines of streets; lights flickering on. Traffic lights changed from green to red. Cars and shops, my school and its playing fields, our old house. My life laid out on a map, waiting to be bombed.

It came to me suddenly. A truth so real and obvious that my legs nearly buckled under me. If I didn't solve the trail, then my dad was going to prison. End of story. If I didn't find all the clues and follow them to the end, he was going to be branded a traitor and he was going to prison *for life*.

The words from Lily's notebook tumbled in my head.

I have to save my dad. If only I can break the code.

All those years ago, she'd been trying to save her dad from something, and here was me trying to save mine. Had she saved him? Well, it was *my* dad who needed saving now, and I was going to do whatever it took. For whatever reason, Dad had decided to use Lily's trail and I was going to get to the end of it and get him home to us. I felt my teeth clench. If it killed me, I was going to get my dad home.

The window was a dark mirror, reflecting back another me: the fingertips of his raised hand pressed tight against mine.

There was a movement in the street that caught my eye. A figure standing there, staring up. A woman in a long, dark coat and hat. But when I looked again, she'd gone.

7

Intruders

It was still snowing as we drove home. Hannah was in the front with the radio turned right up. Mum peered ahead at the road and the red traffic lights, her hands tight on the steering wheel. Her yellow leather bag was on the back seat next to me with the fat envelope sticking from it that Mr Edwards had given her as we left.

The seat belt pressed uncomfortably on my ribs. I was knackered but I felt wide awake. That figure I'd seen looking up had really creeped me out. How had she disappeared so quickly? My brain was all jumpy, full of Dad, of what I had to do; of the way he'd used Lily's seventy-year-old trail, rather than one of his own. Was that to keep things more secret?

Big flakes of snow fell and the wipers struggled to keep the windscreen clear, scraping the glass as the music from the radio thudded, all out of time. I stared out in a daze at the stretch of tarmac and the white grass verges lit by the car headlights as we made our way along the windy road away from town.

LION EAGLE. I had to focus on Lily's next clue, peel all the other stuff out of my head and work it out, but it was hard not to think about what Mr Edwards told me, hard not to think about the house being bugged.

The noise of my phone beeping pulled me out of my brooding. I had a text from Sasha: Cmng 2 yrs aftr schl. Ru ok?

Then one from Josh, so they must have been talking: I will be at your house after I have cooked Dad his pizza and emptied the bin. Have you seen the snow? From Josh.

As we were coming to the turn for our lane, a big car sped past us in the other direction, sending grit rattling on to us. It had been too fast to see properly, and Mum and Hannah didn't seem to have noticed, but I sat up, suddenly alert. A car with tinted windows? The same kind that had taken Dad away?

Our car came to a stop on the drive, skidding a bit on the gravel. I unclicked my seat belt and Mum turned off the engine. A cold wind made the letter box lift and clank like there was an invisible ghost hand knocking at the house. Mum put her key in the lock and we went in. Everything looked the same as it always did. I went into the front room, flicking as many switches as I could so the room blazed with light. Still a big fat nothing. I must be getting paranoid.

Hannah tramped upstairs. "Cup of tea," Mum said robotically, like it was the answer to everything. I followed her into the kitchen and watched her put the kettle on and pull three mugs from the cupboard.

I thought about the bugs Mr Edwards had warned me about. I searched around a while, but there was no sign of them anywhere. I imagined Special Services people sitting wearing headphones, listening in on every word. It wasn't a nice feeling. They must have thought bugging the house would help them find out the truth about Dad. But then I was back to that question: if Dad had evidence to prove *other* people were guilty, why didn't he trust the Special Services people and tell them where it was? It was all massively confusing.

Mum's voice pulled me out of my worrying. "Feed Bones, will you, Nathan?"

Where *was* Bones? He'd usually be going crazy by this time, drooling for food and barking at the fridge. I went back into the front room, but his basket was empty. He must be having a big nap somewhere. It was a bit strange, but I guessed he'd come out when he was hungry.

I stooped down to tie my shoelace, feeling Lily's message crinkle in my pocket. A loose feather drifted over the carpet. That's when I caught sight of Bones, and that's when I knew.

He was hidden under the piano stool, crammed in between its thick lion-paw feet, his stomach pressed on the floor and his ears flat back against his head, tufts of fur on his back shuddering. And I knew for sure that someone had been in our house while we were away.

A war poster on the wall moved in a draught, the words **LOOK OUT** wobbling. My spine twitched. My first instinct was to rush in and tell Mum, but I forced myself not to. What was the point of making her and Hannah any more worried than they were already? Anyway, Bones cowering under the piano stool was hardly proof of much, was it?

Had they been to our house again, the Special Services people? That wouldn't make any sense, though. Surely they could barge into Foxglove Cottage whenever they wanted, not have to wait until we were out.

A thought stabbed me. What if it hadn't been Special Services people at all?

I remembered what Mr Edwards had said in his office: *Leon mentioned to me that he was collecting evidence on corrupt members of staff.*

I swallowed. *Corrupt members of staff.*

What if *They* knew Dad had evidence against them? What if they'd come back here to look for it? I felt sweat on my forehead.

I reached under and stroked Bones's trembly ears. Whoever they were, they had no right! Breaking in, scaring us. I straightened up and felt my eyes narrow. They must have left some trace to show what they were up to! I yanked the curtains closed and scanned the room better. The piano and the oak table and the Welsh dresser and the warden's helmet nailed over the fireplace. Everything the same as it should be, except. . .

I went over to the big glass dome by the fireplace. I peered through the glass at the stuffed grey carrier pigeon on its perch, making a nose shape in the dust. One of its eye sockets was empty. I saw the glass-bead eye had fallen in the mess of dried moss at the bottom of the case. How had that happened? I looked over the engraved brass plaque nailed to the stand.

Carrier pigeons were used extensively in wartime and travelled many miles in urgent flight, often in terrible weather, often under fire, on a mission to reach their journey's end.
Many a life was saved by these courageous birds.
Many a messenger bird perished in its quest.

And when I looked carefully at the glass dome, I saw that dust was smeared away near the bottom, like someone had recently lifted the glass.

I stared. I wished I could believe a ghost had done it. There was a chapter in my *Mysteries* book about them. Ghosts who hung out in old houses and moved stuff around. One theory was ghosts were energy left over after someone had died, and they couldn't rest in peace for some reason. I preferred ghosts to the idea of corrupt members of staff sneaking about when we weren't in.

But the glass-eye blunder proved they weren't perfect. Thought they might find Dad's evidence stuffed in the pigeon, did they?

I had a sudden worry. I shouldn't keep Lily's message on me any more, not the first clue of the trail; it could be a disaster if they found that. What if they followed me and searched me or something? I needed a hiding place for it. I briefly thought about putting it back in the secret drawer in my bedroom, but if they'd already searched around the pigeon, if they came back, they shouldn't bother again, right? I carefully lifted the heavy glass dome and placed it on the floor. Then I got Lily's message out of my pocket and put it the bottom of the case, covering it with the moss. I left the pigeon eye lying there, exactly how they'd left it, and then I replaced the dome.

I rubbed my dusty hands on my trousers. Had the people who had broken in left more traces around the house? I carried on checking the room. I found a thick silver envelope half-hidden in the Welsh dresser with Happy Birthday, Nat in Dad's handwriting. I felt a lump in my throat. Dad had written it before he was taken. He usually wasn't anywhere near as organized as that, so did that show he'd known he might be arrested? Wiping the glass clean on the attic room window, clearing the milestone of grass and soil . . . preparing something for my birthday on Sunday in case he wasn't here for it. "*Dad*," I whispered to myself. I wondered if there was money in the envelope, and then felt stupid and guilty for even thinking that.

I left Mum in the kitchen and went upstairs, Bones shuffling after me. Hannah was in her room; I heard her laptop keyboard clacking. I went into my bedroom, then Mum and Dad's, while Bones pattered alongside me, his back all hunched and his nose sniffing, but I couldn't see anything out of the ordinary. I heard Hannah come out of her room and the bathroom lock click, then the noise of the shower, so I checked her room out too, even though she'd have gone mad if she'd known I was in there. Nothing to report.

I decided to check the attic library next and went up the spiral staircase, Bones clattering after me on the bare wooden steps. There was a layer of snow on the skylight and I weaved through the gloom and the junk piles to switch on the lamp. The tassels shook, making spider legs of light scuttle up the flowery wallpaper and the old photos hanging there in frames. I looked around awhile before I realized it would be pretty much impossible to work out if anyone had been snooping around in all this mess.

I found myself looking at the photos. There were some young versions of Auntie Hilda, and lots of people I didn't know, all with labels at the bottom of the pictures in the same tiny, neat handwriting in curly black ink. I peered close to read a few.

Hilda with Auntie Susie and Auntie Sarah,
Oxford, 1949...
Hilda Vane with her mother (Ethel) and father
(Peter), 1942...

Bones nuzzled my leg, and I patted his fur.

My eye was drawn to the photo in the furthest corner: a woman wearing a long, dark coat and an army-type hat, standing with a bike. I read the label, and then went even closer to read it again in case my eyes were playing tricks.

Lily Kenley, 1940. BP, Hut 6

The doorbell went, *Match of the Day* style, making me bump into the mannequin and knock off one of its arms.

I struggled to reattach it. "Get that, will you, Nathan?" I heard Mum bellow. "I'm busy!"

I sprinted down the stairs, my brain in a tangle. *Lily Kenley. 1940. BP. Hut 6.* Bletchley Park? There were buildings there called huts and they all had numbers; I remembered from our school trip. Now here was a link between the Bletchley Park on the milestone and Lily – it *must* be where her trail went next!

"Friday the eleventh of November, five eighteen p.m.," Josh called through the letter box, so I knew he was stressed. I went and opened the front door. Sasha was with him.

"Sorry we're late," said Sasha as she stamped the snow

off her shoes in the hall and took off her coat in the front room. "But the bus didn't come, so my mum picked us up and wanted to go to Tesco on the way and she was taking *ages*, and then she decided she needed a new pair of shoes for winter – you know how she is – so we had to stop at a shoe place, and we ended up getting Josh a pair as well."

"Yes, sorry." Josh sat down and smiled sheepishly as he lifted his tatty trouser leg to show me a gleaming pair of trainers. "They're water impermeable, luminous and aerodynamic, with high-technology cushioned rubber soles and an excellent tread. Sorry."

"Anyway," Sasha said, "my dad'll come and pick us up later, to save us walking back in the dark. Any news?"

I shook my head. It was too hard to tell them about my dad. Even if I wanted to, me thinking about bugs being everywhere, like scuttling, dirty little insects with enormous ears . . . that image was just too much.

Josh took off his woolly hat and his hair stood on end with static. He stared at me, wide-eyed. "You don't know what he's been arrested for yet?"

I shrugged, trying to look like it was no big deal. "We went to see his solicitor. But he didn't say much."

I heard Mum clattering about in the kitchen, still in robot mode most likely. I heard the radiators trying to clang into action like they were in competition with each other.

Josh rubbed his nose with a frown.

"You *still* don't know what he's been arrested for!" said

Sasha. "If I were you, I'd be going crazy!"

I thought about Mr Edwards telling us about Dad and the Prevention of Terrorism Act; about the chance he'd be sentenced to life in prison. "He didn't say much," I repeated, my voice shaky. Bones whimpered from his basket and curled back into an uneasy sleep, his back twitching. I tried to switch topics. "How was school?" I asked.

"OK," said Sasha, shrugging and giving me a funny look. *Stupid!* Like anyone asks that, except parents. She'd know straightaway I was trying to change the subject. She probably knew I wasn't telling her everything.

"The teachers beat us in the football match," Josh said mournfully. "Miss Mussi scored a hat-trick." He sneezed and put his hat back on and opened a bag of crisps. "I can help you get a fire going if you want," he crunched. "It's unfriendly, having a cold house."

Sasha shoved Josh in the ribs and pulled a face at me, trying to get me to laugh. "Subtle as ever, Joshua."

I smiled back. It felt good to smile. Weird. Wrong, what with the stuff going on with Dad. I had to work out the lion eagle clue! I *had* to get to Bletchley Park – first thing in the morning, as soon as it opened!

Josh frowned. "Oh. Sorry." He shoved in another crisp. "What happened to the pigeon?"

Trust Josh to notice! I bent down by the grate and took some coils of newspaper from the basket. Sasha screwed her face up at the bird's empty eye socket. "Strange the solicitor couldn't tell you *anything* about your dad, Nathan."

Now it was her turn to be subtle. I piled up more paper coils. *Keep Sasha and Josh out of it*, I told myself.

"Yes, it is puzzling," said Josh. "But I don't get a good feeling about any of this business. Not at all."

I shoved a white firelighter cube into the pile of newspaper. *Don't tell them anything*, I said to myself. *You must not say a thing.* "Mmmm," I said, keeping my head turned away.

I spun the wheel of the lighter and held the flame to the cube. The edges lit and turned black, and then the paper caught and I built a pyramid of twigs over it.

Sasha came closer. I felt her eyes on me. "You can tell us, Nathan. We're not going to blab to anyone, you know."

"No," said Josh, looking hurt. "Course we won't."

"You'd better not," I said. The words came out all fierce. I didn't mean them to. I dumped a chunk of wood on the growing fire, feeling the heat on my face.

"Nathan," said Sasha gently. "What is it?"

"We'll help you any way we can," said Josh, and I knew he meant it. We always stuck up for each other. Ever since primary school when we'd been put on the same table. I looked at my friends, and suddenly it all felt too much to keep in any more. I couldn't help it. I felt my face start to crumple.

"Tell us, Nathan," said Sasha quietly, and she was close

to me with her hand on my arm and I could smell that vanilla kind of smell in her hair.

"Nathan?" said Josh, his face all serious and upset.

I dropped another log on the fire and watched the flames curl up the wood. I waited until it was properly alight. I swallowed. Then I told them. Nothing the people listening wouldn't know already; I told them what Dad could be charged with and that he could go to prison for life, and after I'd said it relief slapped over me like a wave, leaving me shivering.

Sasha gasped. "But that's terrible, Nathan."

"I saw that on telly once," said Josh, wide-eyed. "Someone was pinching files off a top-secret computer and selling them for loads of money."

Josh watches a lot of that kind of crime stuff on the telly. Thanks to his hopeless dad, he watched a lot of telly in general.

"But why would they think it was your dad, Nathan?" said Sasha. "He would *never* do anything like that!"

I said nothing. The rest was a secret. Dad's and mine. I'd promised. I stabbed the fire with a poker. I definitely couldn't tell them any more, bugs or no bugs. I stared at the flames a while so I didn't have to look at them.

"What's this?" asked Josh. I turned slowly and it took me a few seconds to register what he was flapping about in his hand. "Who's Lily?" he asked way too loudly. "Why does she need help?"

I leapt up and tried to snatch the paper back, but he'd

read it. He'd only gone and read it! My jaw went tight. I felt sick. Great idea, Nathan, to put the message in with the pigeon! Why did Josh have to be so *nosy*?

"But this Lily," Josh went on. "We need to find her and. . ."

I clamped Josh's mouth with my hand and he fell back on to the settee in surprise. Sasha looked at me in shock. "Take it easy, Nathan. I read it as well!"

I gestured wildly for them to be quiet. They'd read the first clue! They'd both read it! My stomach twisted up. Worse than that, Josh had said: *Who's Lily? Why does she need help? We need to find her.* If the bugs had picked that up. . . I'd have to pray they hadn't.

I went to close the door between us and Mum in the kitchen, and then I turned on the telly and remote-controlled the volume up. I gestured them closer, mouthing over the noise. "The house is bugged."

I jabbed a finger at the date on the message, and Josh's mouth formed an "O" shape and he stayed sitting there gripping a cushion. "I was only trying to sort out your pigeon," he said as the telly blared. "It was disturbing."

But now Sasha and Josh knew.

Would Dad be upset when he found out? He'd said it had to be our secret. That the more people who knew, the more dangerous it was. Would he think I'd let him down? I would have kept it secret, though, I was sure I would have.

I crouched back by the fire. I prodded the flames and sparks sprayed up. Dad said we couldn't trust anyone,

I thought miserably. I imagined him, an old man in a prison cell.

And then – maybe it was the way Josh was rocking and staring around for secret devices and looking so worried, or the way Sasha was resting her head on my shoulder, and maybe it was just because I was rubbish at keeping secrets, and they knew the first clue now anyway – but I hunted out a big pad of lined paper and a pen and I started to write.

I wrote about Dad collecting evidence on people at his work, and about Lily's strange trail, right up to the last clue on the milestone, and my theory that Lily had worked at Bletchley Park – all in brief, obviously, or it would have been a novel, and it took me ages as it was – and how I had to get to the end of the trail because I thought it would lead to the evidence. I explained how Mum and Hannah hadn't been told anything

AND SHOULD NOT BE TOLD!!!!! DAD SAID IT WAS DANGEROUS.

I wrote about the car with tinted windows and Mr Edwards and the bugs and the figure I thought had been watching me, and about the pigeon's eye and how I knew someone had broken into the house.

They read as I wrote, saying nothing, and they stayed really still and wide-eyed for quite a while after I'd finished. They were trying to take it all in, I guess. I stared at the pages of writing on the pad on my knee. It *would* have made a good book, if it hadn't all been true.

I ripped the pages off the pad and screwed them into a ball and tossed it on the fire. I slapped the notepad shut and flung down my pen. My fingers were killing me from gripping the pen so tensely and pressing on the paper so hard. I hid Lily's message back in the bottom of the glass dome, thinking I'd find a better hiding place for it later. "Let's go in the garden." I gestured with my thumb and clicked off the telly. The noise was doing my head in.

"But I was just getting warm!" whispered Josh, as Sasha pulled her coat back on and dragged him out.

We stood on the lawn by the rusty air-raid shelter with its sprinkling of moonlit snow, stamping about in the cold, but well away from any bugs, I hoped.

Sasha gripped my arm, bubbling with questions. "Someone broke into your house? Who do you think it was? What were they after?"

I told them my theory about corrupt members of staff at my dad's work.

"Bound to be!" said Josh, all scared-looking. "I saw a film about that once. Yes, *They* need to find the evidence as soon as they can, and *destroy* it!"

Sasha hugged herself tight. "What do you think the evidence is – a big folder of papers or something? How come your dad didn't give it to Mr Edwards?" she said. "Or just tell him where it is? Surely he trusts his own solicitor!"

"I don't know," I said. "I thought that too. There's something weird going on there."

"The corrupt staff got to him, probably," said Josh, and we turned to look at him. "They probably threatened to, you know, do nasty things to his family or something. Your dad could have known the corrupt staff would threaten Mr Edwards, maybe bribe him with money, but threats are easier. That's why your dad didn't want to tell him where the evidence was."

I thought that through. What Josh was saying – it made sense. I remembered the way Mr Edwards had looked nervously at the photos of his kids on his desk – what had he said again in his office? Something about finding your weak spots. . . *They find your weak spots*, that was it. *Apply pressure*. They'd threatened him, that must be it, and Dad must have guessed they had.

"Mr Edwards warned you, though, Nathan," said Sasha, "so he can't be all bad, right? I'm not sure I'd trust him totally, though.

"But there's something I really don't get," she continued with a frown. "These Special Services people who are investigating all this. They're part of the Ministry of Defence, right? They're just going on the information they have about your dad to get a prosecution. They're only trying to find out the truth, surely."

I nodded hard. "At the moment they think Dad's making stuff up, but they'd investigate everything, wouldn't they?" I said. "Every little thing. If it's so important to national security and all that; if soldiers were killed. . ."

I stopped dead; felt my mouth clamp shut. Sasha stared at me, shocked. "*Soldiers died?*"

"Yeah," I mumbled. I hadn't told them that bit yet. It still made me feel sick, just thinking about it.

We went quiet. I jabbed a toe in the snow.

"So as I was saying." Sasha cleared her throat. "These Special Services people. All they want to do is find out if your dad's guilty and if anyone else is involved. If they had the evidence, they'd see your dad wasn't to blame and they'd release him. So why is he so worried about telling them where the evidence is, or even what it is? It makes him look like he's got things to hide."

I felt that same shiver of worry. Even if we found the evidence, what might it say about Dad? Might he get into more trouble?

"Maybe your dad *can't* say anything," said Josh quietly.

We stared at him.

"Maybe he knows that some of the people questioning him are corrupt too," Josh continued. "Had you thought of that? It's not too unlikely." He hopped about, his new trainers shining in the moonlight. "I watched this programme once – *True Crimes: Traitors*!"

"If it *is* true there's dodgy people in the Special Services as well as the Ministry of Defence," said Sasha breathlessly, "your dad would definitely keep his mouth shut about the evidence, Nathan."

"OK. Let's think this through." Josh started pacing about, half talking to himself. Tree branches creaked against each other in the wind. "OK, your dad works in a place where there's loads of really secret information, and imagine one day he accidentally finds out that someone in his department is doing something wrong, like selling classified army files." Josh blew on his hands. "But your dad knows he can't just accuse people like that. He needs evidence."

I remembered Dad's words to me before they took him. *Without evidence we've got nothing.* Mr Edwards had pretty much said the same thing.

Sasha opened her mouth to speak, but Josh was on a roll. "But once the corrupt staff knew Nathan's dad was on to them, they'd want to know exactly what he'd found out. Your house could have been bugged for days, Nathan!"

"We have to get rid of those bugs straightaway!" cut in Sasha.

Josh shook his head hard. "Even if we *could* find them, if we did that They'd know we were on to them! No, the only thing the corrupt staff would want to do now is destroy all the evidence Nathan's dad collected that proves they're guilty, and then. . . Oooh!" He put a hand either side of his face. "If they don't want to just kill Nathan's dad and make it look like an accident. . ."

Kill Dad? My panic levels soared.

". . .they'd probably try and make it look like *he* did the secrets-selling instead!" continued Josh excitedly. "They'd try and *frame* him — that's it! They found out Nathan's dad got to know what they were up to, and now they want to frame him so *he* gets the blame instead of them!"

Me and Sasha looked at each other. Was all this just Josh's overactive imagination? The result of spending way too long in front of the telly? I had to admit, though, it fitted.

"Hang on, Josh. Hang on," said Sasha. "These corrupt staff or whoever, how would they make it look like Nathan's dad did it?"

Josh shrugged. "Plant evidence . . . twist evidence . . . destroy evidence. . . It would have to be someone high up at work for Mr Vane to be that worried. He would have just gone to his bosses at the Ministry of Defence otherwise. It has to be someone with a lot of power. There could be a whole group of them." His eyeballs glinted. There could be a whole network of corrupt members of staff, not just people at the Ministry of Defence and Special Services. There could be police, too, even, all in it for the money. We could be talking millions, if they've been selling military secrets to foreign governments. Then there'd be no one you could tell!"

"So everyone is in on it, are they?" said Sasha with a short laugh. "The entire police force too!"

"No, course not!" said Josh. "But how would you know who to trust? It'd be better not to trust anyone and not to tell anyone anything."

I heard Dad's voice in my head: *You can't trust anyone,*

you hear me? Don't trust anyone. Was Josh right? Was that why Dad wanted me to follow Lily's trail; why he didn't just give the Special Services the evidence straight? Because he couldn't know for sure who was corrupt and who wasn't? If Dad didn't know who to trust, how the heck would I?

"First of all, Nathan's dad has to check he has all the evidence, watertight," said Josh. "And then he has to make sure the evidence gets to the *right* person, because if it gets to the *wrong* person then that person will destroy it, or frame him with it."

"I get it!" Sasha clapped excitedly at him. "Josh, you're a genius!"

He went red. "Who says television is bad for young minds?" he mumbled. "But it's just an idea," he added, and he hunched his shoulders and opened another bag of crisps. According to him, crunching was calming.

Sasha held on to me. "We really, *really* need to work out this lion eagle clue, Nathan," she said.

"I know that," I said, stomping the snow flat. "We need to get to Bletchley Park as soon as it opens tomorrow and. . ." I stopped. My heart rattled against my ribs. There had been a noise in the bushes, a rustling. I strained my ears to hear. I felt Sasha and Josh tense up beside me. Suddenly a shape shot out and across the lawn. A fox. Just a fox.

I breathed out in relief and we all laughed nervously.

"If the evidence really is at the end of the trail," said

Sasha, "then your dad had to hide it somewhere he was sure it wouldn't be found. He'd have known the house would get searched." She clicked her fingers. "Then why not use clues from an old trail he'd already cracked? Clever!"

It was just what I'd thought. Lily's seventy-year-old trail. Nobody would easily think to follow that.

"Here's the government people thinking they were being all precise and thorough and searching everywhere, but they'd just not see the clues," laughed Sasha. "They wouldn't be interested in a load of old stuff from the nineteen forties. Oh, we *so* have to get to Bletchley Park and solve the lion eagle clue!"

Bones started barking from the house. I saw him at the back room window and we heard his muffled yowls from where we were standing, so he must have been loud. Paws up on the glass. Claws scratching. Bones never barked much. It took him all his energy just to move about. There was another fox, maybe? I glanced about the garden, but I couldn't see anything. Even so, it made me twitchy.

I saw Hannah appear at the dark window and pull him away by the collar. She peered at us through the glass and gave me a suspicious look. I guess we must have looked weird, the three of us, standing there like that in the freezing garden in the moonlight. She scowled and closed the curtain.

Josh fiddled with the end of his scarf. "You do realize that if the corrupt staff get to know about the trail and that *you* know about it, they might get heavy, like. . ."

He glanced at the back room window. ". . .like try and warn you off by killing your dog! Or try and stop you by breaking both your legs. Or force you to tell them everything using torture methods," he said in a scared whisper. "Or they would let you lead them to the end of the trail and find the evidence and then *pounce!*" he hissed, hugging himself.

Sasha rolled her eyes at him. I glanced into the shadowy spaces between the trees where someone could be watching. A bird cawed in a tree and all three of us jumped.

Sasha clutched my hand. "Listen, Nathan, you've told us and we're in this together now, OK? We'll help you with the trail and we won't say a single word to anyone. Right, Josh?"

"I agree we don't tell anyone," said Josh anxiously.

He laid his fingers on top of ours and I felt the warmth of both their hands over mine. "Thanks," I managed.

But I couldn't help feeling worried – had it been a mistake to tell Sasha and Josh? What Josh had said about the corrupt staff getting to know we were on the trail – had I put them in danger? Dad's words kept nagging at me: *The more people who know, the more dangerous it is.*

"Tell me everything about the clues you found, Nathan, please!" Josh had gone all hyper again and was pacing the garden, leaving footprints with an excellent tread in the snow. "I'm really not good with patience."

So I told them, before Josh did himself an injury. About

the eye scratched in the attic library and the clue on the bottom of the bucket, and Sasha and me had to grab hold of Josh's arms to stop him running to the well to wind up the bucket right there and then as I was telling him that part.

"So once we're at Bletchley Park," I said, "we get to Hut 6 and. . ."

I paused. I'd heard another noise. From the shadowy bushes close by. Something like twigs shifting; leaves crackling as if someone had ever so gently stepped on them. Josh had gone horribly pale. I lowered myself down and picked up a little rock; it was all I could find.

"Who's there?" I called.

Silence.

I took a step in the direction the sound had come from.

"Who's there?" I said again.

8

Lily Kenley

I took another step forward. All the hairs at the back of my neck shivered. Someone was there, I could feel it.

I felt my fists go tight on the rock I was holding. I could hear Sasha and Josh behind me, shuffling through the snow.

I peered hard into the gloom between spindly bushes and tree trunks.

And then, for a single, tiny second, there was a dark shape lurching out from the shadows in front of me, a figure, a flurry of movement, a flapping coat, someone running away, and I held up the rock and charged after them with a cry, and Sasha and Josh were screaming and running too.

But the figure was gone.

We scoured the garden three times before we were sure. We found footprints in the snow, but when we tried to follow the tracks, they kept bringing us right back in a loop. Whoever it was had completely disappeared.

We huddled together on the lawn, panting and trembling. Could it have been a corrupt member of staff? How much had they overheard? I desperately tried to remember everything we'd said since Bones started barking. He must have known they were there, I realized; seen them moving. I pulled off a glove and gnawed my nails. We'd not said anything about Lily, I didn't think, but we'd talked about the trail. I felt my jaw go tight. We'd definitely talked about the trail, and Bletchley Park.

"Let's get back in," I said shakily.

We hurried into the house and bolted the door and went to the front room and made the fire really big and sat close together on the settee in front of it with the pad of paper. I could hear Mum, still in the kitchen, and music thudded through the ceiling from Hannah's room.

What had happened had happened, I told myself with a grimace. We just had to get on; be way more careful.

LION EAGLE I scribbled at last, when my hand had stopped shaking enough. ?????

?????? wrote Josh.

Sasha wrote: If we knew more about Lily, it might help us with the clue. Was she your relative?

Don't think so. Wait. I rushed up to the attic library and came down with Lily's notebook and the photo of her from the wall. I wriggled back into my place on the settee as Sasha fingered the caption. *Lily Kenley. 1940. BP, Hut 6.*

Josh wrote: I don't remember seeing Hut 6 on our school trip, do you?

Sasha and I shook our heads. If only Bletchley Park wasn't closed, I thought; if only we could have gone there right there and then. I even felt like breaking in; this waiting about was a nightmare! But Sasha was right; we may as well use the time to find out more about Lily; try and get a breakthrough with the lion eagle clue before we checked out Hut 6 tomorrow.

I remembered something Dad had said to me that night. What was it again? *She lived in this house.* I put the photo of Lily on the mantelpiece and gestured for Sasha and Josh to wait again. I went to the hall cabinet and pulled open the drawer. It was still there, the book I'd seen when I was looking for my head torch last night, the guest book with its broken black leather cover. I brought it into the front room and we squashed back up to look inside. The first name in there was someone called Josie Johnson with the date August 1929.

Wow! Goes way back. This house must have been a B&B or something. Look at all the people who stayed here.

Nice tidy room. . . Josh tapped at the entry and licked his lips. *Apricot cheesecake to die for.*

I turned the pages and we scrolled down the lists of names, until, at last, there it was, the name I'd been hoping to find.

Lily Kenley. February 1939. The comments space was blank.

"She signed in but never signed out," Josh whispered,

and he glanced around the room as if he expected to see her standing right there.

Lily looked at me from the mantelpiece. *What happened to you?* I thought about her message; the date on it, *November 1940.*

She stayed here nearly 2 years! I wrote on the pad. Probably while she was working at BP.

I heard the phone ring and Mum answered it in the kitchen. Sasha pointed at Lily's notebook with a questioning look. I showed her – I have to save my dad. If only I can break the code – and the weird lists of capital letters in threes, crossed neatly through: ~~BBC BBD BBE~~. . . What exactly did Lily have to save her dad *from*?

Josh jumped up, scribbling and looking super excited, and we had to grab the pad off him to see what he'd written.

Hut 6 = Enigma code BUT – he tapped the strings of letters – this isn't Enigma code. Enigma code needs FIVE capital letters, not just THREE.

We'd learnt about Enigma code on a school trip – we'd seen the special machines at Bletchley Park, the Enigma Machines that were used by the Nazis to write secret messages. Josh was crazy about that kind of stuff! He would have stolen an Enigma Machine to take home if he'd had the chance.

He tugged my arm and wrote: Lion eagle could be an anagram. He scribbled down the letters over his page – L I O N E A G L E – and started to play around with them. ANGLE he wrote, then ANGEL, then ALIEN LEGO, which I'm not sure was really helping.

The kitchen door swung open and I just had time to screw up the page we'd been writing on and toss it on the fire before Mum clattered in with a tray of three steaming mugs and plates of sandwiches and chocolate biscuits. "Hi, kids," she said brightly, but she looked all pale and I saw her mascara had run on one eye. "You're all being very quiet and secretive in here."

I sat back and tried to smile, but I saw the carrier pigeon staring at me from its eyeless socket and I couldn't get comfy on the settee any more. "Who was it on the phone?" I asked. I felt the edge of Lily's notebook jabbing me from under a knitted cushion. "Anything about Dad?"

"No . . . yes, but he's fine," Mum said, a bit too fast. "Mr Edwards was just saying how he's doing. He's fine. No change."

She was lying. I could tell.

Josh smiled nervously. "Want one, Mrs Vane?" He held a newly opened bag of crisps out to her. "They're salt and vinegar."

"No thanks, Josh."

"I'm . . . I'm sorry about Mr Vane," said Sasha.

Mum put the tray in front of the fire. She forced a smile. "Thought you might be hungry."

"I always am," said Josh. "Thanks."

But we couldn't carry on the conversation any more because Mum stayed in the room chatting about everything *except* Dad and then we heard a car on the drive and Sasha's dad beeping to pick up her and Josh.

93

"We'll try and have the clues cracked by Sunday," Sasha whispered in my ear at the door. "Then we can celebrate by having a big party for your birthday!"

She gave me a hug and Josh shook my hand. I felt that surge of hope again, Dad's trust in me. Then the dread, like cement setting hard on my chest.

"You should get to bed, Nathan," said Mum when they'd gone and I'd bolted the door again and put on the chain.

"But it's only half seven." I prodded the fire with the poker and made it flare.

"You need to get some sleep!" she snapped, all stressed. "Catch up on last night."

The phone rang again and Mum went to answer it. I got Lily's notebook from under the settee cushion and climbed upstairs with it hidden under my jumper. I stopped on the landing and looked out through an edge of curtain, checking the lane for dodgy cars with tinted windows, or shapes lurking in the shadows. Nothing, but I couldn't help feeling nervous after what had happened in the garden. Had it been the people trying to frame Dad? I thought again of the figure outside Mr Edwards's office with a shudder. Who knew if they were still around. They could be back any time.

I got ready for bed and climbed in while Bones scrambled up, his stumpy tail thumping the duvet as he got comfy. Good old Bones.

I stroked his head and started flicking through Lily's notebook again. I was about to call it a day when I came across something I'd missed the first time, something that made me sit right up in bed: something written sideways in the margin in really tiny letters.

10th Nov 1940
Is Coventry the target? It must be close now. I have to break the Enigma and cannot rest until then.

So Josh was right! It *was* Enigma codes Lily had been working on. That didn't explain the sets of three letters instead of five, but still. Coventry, though? That was never mentioned in our school trip to Bletchley Park. What was all that about?

My mind went into overdrive. I listened to work out whether Mum was still downstairs and likely to come up to check I was in bed anytime soon. I heard her on the phone, her voice raised but muffled, and I pulled out my laptop and opened up Google. I typed *enigma* into the search box. There was an Oxford Dictionary definition:

---

enigma /i-**nig**-muh/ •**n**. a mysterious or puzzling person or thing.
– ORIGIN Greek *ainigma* "riddle"

Well, the whole thing was puzzling all right. I typed *enigma* and *bletchley park* and found some stuff I already knew:

*First invented by a German engineer, **Enigma** Machines were used in the Second World War to send secret messages. . .*

I clicked to another site.

*Lots of houses in the local area were commissioned to take people who worked at **Bletchley**. Many came from the universities of Cambridge or Oxford. Mathematicians, linguists, physicists, scholars, even musicians. Some of the most brilliant minds in cryptography came together to find ways to break the enemy's secret codes.*

"Crypt-o-graphy," I muttered. It sounded like something to do with dead people rather than code cracking. I typed fast into the search box:

coventry, enigma, bletchley park

103,001 results!

I quickly scanned down the list.

*The **Coventry** Blitz: The real story of the bombing*
*Did Churchill allow the **Coventry** bombing? The myth put to rest*
***Bletchley Park** workers to be honoured by government*

I clicked on the first one and started to read.

In full moonlight on the night of 14th November 1940. . .

Weird. November the fourteenth. This coming Monday. I shivered at the coincidence and carried on reading.

*...509 Luftwaffe bombers attacked **Coventry**... These started a firestorm which devastated most of the city centre... Many buildings were destroyed and 568 people killed...*

*...**Bletchley Park** decoded an **Enigma** message on 11th November that warned a huge raid was coming, code name Moonlight Sonata. It was suspected there were three possible targets: Birmingham, **Coventry** or London, and **Bletchley** were working round the clock to try and find out which city it was.*

My mind whirred. *Firestorm . . . 568 people killed . . . Moonlight Sonata. . .* I thought about Lily's words again. *Is Coventry the target?*

"Nathan!" Mum shouted up. "Your light's not still on, is it?"

The 10th of November, 1940, Lily's question had been dated. It was a bit of a leap, but could Lily's dad have been living in Coventry at the time? Was that why she was so mad about breaking the Enigma code, to know which city was going to be bombed?

"Nathan!" I heard Mum's feet on the stairs. I snapped my laptop closed and flicked the light off, wriggling under my covers.

But couldn't Lily have told her dad to leave, just in case?

My door opened a crack and then closed again, making the model planes move about. They circled slowly in the moonlight, spreading long shadows over the ceiling. I yawned a huge yawn and struggled to think and stay awake. Had Lily saved her dad? What did all this have to do with my dad? What did it have to do with the trail? I had no idea.

My mobile buzzed and I sleepily brought up the text from Sasha. We'll b round asap 2moro & go to bp on bus s x

I settled back into bed. *Lion eagle. . . Lion eagle. . .* I felt my eyelids getting heavier and heavier. I had to think. I had to get to Bletchley Park. I had to work it out. . . But I couldn't keep my eyes open, and then there was Lily in my head, and I vaguely remembered I'd left her photo on the mantelpiece where anyone could find it. . . But my mind was closing inwards like a box lid snapping shut, and there was Lily, looking at me and nodding as she rode her bike away.

9
Bletchley Park

I bolted awake. Bletchley Park!

There was a strange yellow light coming through the curtains like the colour of old paper, and when I drew them back I saw that the snow had got thicker in the night. It covered the pointy roof of the well and the air-raid shelter was a bump of white. I thought about the figure who'd been hiding in the garden, knowing about the trail, knowing where we were heading to next.

The house was deathly quiet. I got dressed under the covers to try and keep warm, and then I tiptoed downstairs. I went into the kitchen and grabbed a few biscuits from the tin and swigged some freezing milk straight from the fridge. *MMXII* spelt the fridge magnets. *MCMXL*, like some random strings of Enigma code rather than the Roman numeral dates Dad and me had made up.

As I turned round with the carton, there was someone

standing in the doorway, and I got such a shock that I let out a yell, splattering milk all over.

"For goodness' sake, Nathan! Who did you think it was?" Mum wiped splashes of milk off her nurse's uniform. She dumped her yellow leather work bag on the table and sloshed some water from the tap into the kettle.

"Sorry." I dabbed at the spilled milk on the table with a piece of kitchen roll. "You going into work today?"

"I had some things to do first," she said vaguely. "Read some legal stuff Mr Edwards sent. . ." Her voice trailed off. She fiddled with some papers in an agitated way. I saw a couple of envelopes with *CRIMINAL JUSTICE SYSTEM* stamped on them in red. A leaflet called *HM Prison Service – Support for Families*. . . She shoved them into her bag and zipped it closed. "Yes, then I'm on the rota for a Saturday shift."

We went into the front room and I stood by the window and checked my watch. When would Sasha and Josh be here? I wished they'd hurry up. Mum paced and sipped her tea. She was being strangely quiet.

My mobile buzzed. Probably Sasha or Josh at last. I sat down on the settee and flipped open the cover. One text message. I clicked on the icon and nearly fell on the floor.

07700900583
This is lily.
Contact me. We. . .

I stared at the message with its ghost-green letters.

Lily?

Lily was texting me?

I could hardly read the next bit, my hand was shaking that badly.

> . . . have to be careful. My
> number's changed. Get in touch.

"Who was that from?" Mum asked as I flipped the cover closed.

"Er . . . just Josh," I said. I took a big slurp from my mug.

A thought rocked me. *Could* Lily Kenley be still alive? How old would that make her? I remembered her date of birth, pencilled in the front of her notebook – *1902* – and did the calculation fast. Over a hundred and ten! It was possible, but not very likely. Could the text be from *another* Lily? Could it be a wrong number?

If Lily hadn't sent it, who had? I remembered Josh's outburst after he'd found the message: *Who's Lily? Why does she need help? We need to find her.* The bugs could have picked that up nice and clear. Was whoever had sent it expecting me to text them back? There was no way I was doing that!

I clicked on the radio and my fingers were still shaking as I turned the music up. "Is it all right if I go to Bletchley Park this morning?" I asked by Mum's ear. "With Sasha and Josh? It's for a class project."

Maybe Mum thought I shouldn't be bothering with school projects and going off with friends and all that kind of stuff, not with how things were with Dad, but she just nodded and I took another big swig of tea. I rubbed my hand over my mouth, trying to push away the text message and the fear prickling over my skin. I looked at my watch again. *Where were Sasha and Josh?*

"How did *this* get on the mantelpiece?"

I could have died! Mum stood there with the photo of Lily in her hand. I remembered I'd gone and left it there, hadn't I? *Stupid or what?*

My teeth clenched as I thought about the bugs and I turned the radio up even more. They might know about the trail and about Bletchley Park, but I wasn't going to let them find out any more about Lily. "Er, I found it in the attic library." I was thinking fast. "It's for the school project I told you about."

"Lily Kenley," muttered Mum, reading the label. "Your dad did tell me once that Auntie Hilda mentioned her a few times. Let me think. What was it your dad said?" She sat down with the photo.

"It's OK, Mum," I said. "Tell me later."

"That was it. . ." she went on. "Hilda didn't know much because she was just a little girl at the time, but she said Lily stayed with them awhile." She tapped the glass in an agitated way as she tried to remember the details. "Turn that music down, can't you? I can't hear myself think! That was it – Lily's mum was dead, your dad said, killed in a London bombing. Brother too. Lily's dad was posted somewhere, as a fireman or something."

Lily's family all dead, all except her dad? Lily looked up at me from her photo on the kitchen table, her eyes pinning me, and I felt suddenly sad; really sad for her.

But there was no time for Lily's story now!

"She boarded with them for a while," went on Mum. "Kept herself to herself, I gathered. Anyway, Hilda told Dad that Lily read her bedtime stories, and played the piano for her, the same piece, over and over and over. Then one morning Lily was gone, and that was the last Hilda ever heard of her."

Hilda and her parents, I thought, they couldn't have known about Lily's message, then. Lily had hidden it too well for that.

My mobile buzzed and I fumbled to read the message in case it was from Lily again. I nearly dropped the phone, my hands were that slippery with sweat.

On way now with josh meet at stop. Sash

I let my heart rate settle. Finally. "I need to meet Sasha and Josh," I said to Mum, getting up. "See you later."

"Before you set off, Nathan." Mum clicked off the radio and she held on to my arm and didn't let go. *Don't mention Lily*, I prayed. *They'll hear you.* But I needn't have worried about that. Something way worse was coming.

Mum looked at me as if she didn't know how to start.

"Hannah knows already," she said, "I told her last night. She stayed over at Gavin's. . . Anyway . . . I wanted to tell you too, but. . . There's been a bit more news." She paused to wipe some hair from her face like she didn't want to go on. It was going to be more bad news, it had to be. The skin on my face went tight.

Mum's words rattled out like bullets. "They're going to formally charge your dad." She gave a strange little laugh. "On Monday morning. Then they'll transfer him out of the area, to a more secure unit further south. We're not allowed to know where." She gnawed at one of her nails and there was a speck of blood on her finger.

I just stood there like a dummy. But today was Saturday! Monday was two days away. *Two days!* "But the solicitor said the situation was stable!" I blurted.

"This is all just intimidation tactics," Mum muttered angrily to herself. "They'll be arresting *me* next!" She stroked my hair. "He's innocent, Nathan," she said. But was that a wobble I heard in her voice?

I didn't know what to say, so I hugged her and then grabbed my coat from the hallway and pulled on my hat and gloves. I left the house and checked up and down the deserted lane. I went as fast as I could on the soft snow heading for the bus stop. The trees leaned in from both sides of the road, their bare branches reaching towards me. I saw Sasha and Josh already waiting at the shelter and when I got there I perched on a plastic flip-down seat and stared hard at the timetable. I knew it by heart – the next bus was ten past eight – but I stared at it anyway, just so I could keep my face turned away from Sasha and Josh and I wouldn't have to tell them anything about Monday, because there was no time for getting upset, only getting on with things. Getting to the end of the trail and finding Dad's evidence.

I hacked at the layer of ice with my toe and stared at the grey circles of chewing gum on the pavement while Sasha and Josh flung about their theories on what *lion eagle* meant.

I knew I should have told them about Lily's text, but I didn't want to scare them. What had I got them messed up in?

Sasha stood up and stuck out her arm. The half-empty bus stopped and we got on and went to sit at the back as it pulled away.

I didn't talk much on the journey, only to fill the two of them in on what Mum had said about Lily, and to tell them the stuff I'd found out about Coventry being bombed. I let them carry on discussing *lion eagle* and how we should aim straight for Hut 6, Lily's old hut, when we got to Bletchley Park.

"That's if we ever get there," Sasha said as the bus strained and juddered on the gritted road up the hill towards town.

I cleared a circle on the steamed-up window with the elbow of my coat and watched the snowy fields and spindly trees go past. We got to the edge of Bletchley and

I gazed out at the white pavements and the huddled-up houses. Sasha pressed the bell.

We got off and walked quickly. I couldn't stop thinking about the person in the garden last night and kept glancing behind. I started to have a horrible feeling that someone was following us.

It was nothing I could put my finger on, just half-glimpsed movements reflected in the glass of a telephone box or a shop window as we hurried past, but when I looked back, the street was always deserted.

There was still a way to go. What was I hoping to find when I got to Hut 6? What *did* lion eagle mean? I still had no idea.

We went past a takeaway, past the Dead Duck pub. We walked past a funeral director's with an old-fashioned black clock hanging outside; fanged teeth and fireworks on sale in a shop window; a noodle bar with bits of its shop sign come off so it said *N dies*.

Heavy, strange-coloured clouds swirled in the sky like a storm was on its way, and an icy drizzle blew in my face. A page of a newspaper skittered across the tarmac and stuck against my foot before tumbling on. It had gone weirdly dark. A streetlamp flicked on over me so I had two shadows. A group of kids from school were messing about outside a newsagent's and I recognized a boy from our year.

"Hey! Gnat features!" he called over the noise of traffic. "Isn't that your dad?" He jabbed a finger at the board outside. There was a headline in the criss-crossing diamond shapes and I paused in my walking to let the words sink in.

TRAITOR! LOCAL MAN HELD

My head felt like a lump of lead. Somehow I managed to shake it.

"Yeah it is." The boy darted forward and stood in front of me, his arms folded tightly. "He works at the Ministry of Defence, doesn't he? I read he's been selling army secrets to the enemy! Got our soldiers killed."

I stared at the pavement, at its bits of broken glass and cigarette stubs. I could feel the kids smothering me with bad looks.

"Course it's not him!" said Sasha, pulling at my arm. Her breath spiralled out in clouds. "Don't listen to that idiot," she said to me.

We crossed the main road and headed along a side street, but I still felt I was being watched everywhere I went, and not just by corrupt staff. Now it was like everyone knew my secret. *Your dad's a traitor. Your dad's a traitor.* I felt eyes on me from every window and every street corner. *He's innocent*, I repeated to myself. *Innocent.* A plane flew over and I slipped slightly on the pavement's trodden-down snow.

We got to the entrance of Bletchley Park. "Now remember," I said sternly, "if anyone asks, it's a school project, right?" Josh nodded with a serious look and we approached the gate.

There was a security man reading a newspaper in a

little booth, and I thought with a shudder how he looked a bit like one of those men who'd taken Dad away. "Watch yourselves, kids." He stared at us and then pointed out the entrance. "It's slippy underfoot." When I glanced back, he was still watching us over the top of his paper.

We walked through the car park and up to a building with ADMISSIONS on it. We went in to the main desk and Sasha got our tickets, because her mum always gave her lots of money, and then we craned over the fold-out map we'd been given, looking for Hut 6.

Clusters of buildings spread over the whole site, criss-crossed with wide driveways and little paths. There was the lake and the mansion and the café and the post office, and loads of labels with *Hut Number This* and *Hut Number That*.

"There it is!" Sasha tapped the map. "Let's go!"

We rushed out and along the drive, round one side of the lake where a couple of ducks stood gloomily on the ice. Some of the buildings we passed were all broken-looking; some of them had been done up. We passed a sign that said *Hut 8: Alan Turing's Hut*.

"This can't be it!" I said as we stopped at a nearby hut.

"It is," said Josh, tapping a sign. "*Hut 6*," he read. "*Interpretation Centre: Intelligence and D-Day. . . Awaiting funds for restoration*."

I stared at the long hut with the snow-speckled paint flaking along its plank walls like shed skin and its rusty metal gutters and drainpipes.

"We can't go in." Sasha tried the door, then stood on tiptoe to look in through one of the few grubby windows that wasn't boarded up. "It's all empty anyway."

I peered through the pane. Rubble and rubbish and clods of plaster were strewn over the floor, and nails spilled out from big plastic tubs into spiky pools. A broken hammer, a crooked screwdriver, a rusty saw with half its teeth missing. There were damp stains on the walls, and grey mouldy patches, and old wires hanging like snakes from the ceiling. I tried to imagine Lily working in there. *Anyone* working in there. Seventy years gone by as if they'd never existed.

"Lion eagle. Lion eagle," I muttered. "Keep looking. You check the left side, Josh; I'll do the right side. Sasha, you check the front and back walls."

Nothing, nothing, nothing.

"Where shall we try next?" said Sasha, after twenty minutes of getting nowhere. I heard the edge of disappointment in her voice.

I studied the guide map. This looking around all seemed way too random. "Maybe the mansion? It was the headquarters for all the Bletchley Park stuff, right?"

We hurried along the gravel drive towards a huge house that looked like it was a row of fancy houses stuck together, with a green dome roof at one end and red brick walls, and all these tall windows and chimneys.

A couple of blokes in paint-splattered overalls and hard hats were standing either side of the entrance drinking out of steaming cups and smoking. And there was a stream of foreign kids in green uniforms jostling with us to get in the big front door.

We walked quickly through the rooms, keeping a lookout for any kind of lion or eagle. We stared up at the stained glass roof of something called the anteroom and looked through shelves of books in the library, but we weren't finding anything.

"What's that music?" said Josh. Piano notes drifted through the house, a crackly old classical piece.

"Der, der, der. Der, der, der. Der, der, der. Der, der, der," Josh sang, mimicking the music. "That one? I can't think."

We followed the sound. It was coming out of a part-opened door that said BALLROOM by it, but there was yellow and black tape tied across the entrance like it was a murder scene.

NO ENTRY – DANGER – WORK IN PROGRESS said the tape.

Beyond I could see a big room with a really high ceiling and posh lights like upside-down bells hanging on gold chains, and the walls were completely covered in wooden panels, and there was a tall painters' stepladder planted in the middle and all this scaffolding up the walls and wooden planks to walk on. The floor was covered in sheets, and there were large pots of paint and trays with rollers scattered about.

"Unfortunately the ballroom ceiling is being repainted

110

at the moment," came a voice. A woman was behind us with a guided tour group. "We've kept the music playing, though, to give you a feel for the place." She lowered her voice and went all dramatic. "The story goes that one poor soul on recent late-night cleaning duty heard music playing in here, this very same piece! But when he went to switch the gramophone off, he saw it wasn't turned on! He later found out it hadn't worked in decades." The crowd gave a small gasp, Josh too. The tour guide winked. "Needless to say, the ballroom didn't get vacuumed *that* evening!" There was laughter as the group filed away.

"Do you think that's true?" said Josh, wide-eyed. "About the ballroom being haunted? I saw this programme once where there was a ghost and. . ."

"Let's try to get in," I said. "Have a look around. The ballroom's the only room we haven't checked."

Sasha lifted the tape, about to duck under it.

"Where d'you think you're going?" There was a gruff voice behind us and two workmen stood there, looking really annoyed.

"My mum works here," Sasha lied, "and. . ."

"Not today, she doesn't."

"But she told me to. . ."

The voice got gruffer. "We'll be finished by *Monday*, young lady."

I took another step forward. "If I could just. . ."

The gruff one stood squarely in the doorway and folded

his arms. "Ballroom opens *Monday*, I said. Come back and do your dancing then."

"Good one!" the other man laughed. Then they bobbed under the tape and banged the door shut on us.

Monday. I couldn't wait until Monday! I promised myself I was going to get in there somehow before then.

"Forget the ballroom for now," said Sasha, looking at the map. "How about we try the Exhibition Centre, Block B? It's full of old stuff."

We ended up going out of the mansion as the same loud group of schoolkids were leaving, and got jostled through the door and into the cold air.

We went back the way we'd come, past the lake and back into the building where we'd bought our tickets. There were some stairs near the entrance desk, and we walked down into a big room full of glass cases and displays.

"Excellent!" said Josh, rushing over to a cabinet and peering in. "I thought of something – a lion, that's the symbol of England, and the eagle was the symbol of the Third Reich. It might be something to do with that! Medals, maybe, or coats of arms."

"Keep looking!" I said, getting a bit hopeful, and we dashed about the display cases, staring into them.

"Best not to run about in here. Take a lot of cleaning, those floors do."

I spun round and a man with a grey moustache was standing there. *Percy*, it said on his name badge. *Bletchley Park Volunteer*.

"And careful near that Bombe," he said.

I backed away a step, but Josh grinned. "Not a bomb, Nathan – a *Bombe*!"

I still didn't get them.

Percy chuckled and pointed at a sign over a big metal box-shape with all these coloured dials all over it. THE TURING BOMBE REBUILD PROJECT, the sign said, and I nodded with a slight laugh as I remembered being told about it on our school trip.

"This one's called Phoenix," said Josh. "Look, it says so on that wooden plaque."

"A mythical bird rising from the ashes," said Percy dramatically.

I didn't think the machine looked anything like a phoenix. It was an eagle we needed anyway.

"The Bombe machine did an automatic search to find all the Enigma rotor settings," said Josh excitedly. "So the Bletchley people could work out the enemy messages."

"Knows his stuff, this chap does," Percy said, making Josh blush and grin even more. "Alan Turing was the fella that designed it, building on an originally Polish idea." He pointed out a statue at the other side of the hall of a man sitting working. "That's him there. Clever chap, that one, too."

"Here's an Enigma Machine!" Josh called from a nearby glass display case. "We need to know about this, don't we, Nathan? You know, for our *school project*."

I nodded at him, but I couldn't help thinking we were

113

getting sidetracked. Actually I was itching to ask Percy straight about the lion eagle clue. He didn't *look* corrupt, but how could you tell? And even if we could trust him, he might start spouting at the top of his voice and who knew who might be listening round a corner. No, that would have been way too risky. I jut hoped Josh wouldn't put his foot in it.

"An Enigma Machine, that's right," said Percy, going over and clearing his throat. "One of several captured from the enemy. I'm sure you know it was used by the Nazis to send secret messages."

"What I want to know is how did they keep what they were doing so secret here at Bletchley Park?" asked Josh. He was starting to take the school project cover a bit far. We didn't have time for all these questions!

Percy looked shocked. "Nobody would even *dream* of talking about the work they did here," he said. "Not even to their best mates or families. All the workers at Bletchley had to sign the Official Secrets Act before they started."

I saw Sasha glance at me. I looked at my feet and chewed my lip. I didn't want to hear about the Official Secrets Act. It made me think of Dad, and how he'd been accused of breaking it, though that seemed pretty tame compared to what he was accused of now.

But Percy was on a roll. "Even after the war ended, a lot never let on what they did. Maybe it's hard for us to understand nowadays, that kind of secrecy – saw that statue of a goose yet, did you?" Josh shook his head.

"*The geese that laid the golden eggs but never cackled*, that's what Churchill said the workers at this place were. Even the people living round about didn't know what Bletchley was used for." Percy straightened his back as if he was standing to attention. "Emergency situations call for emergency measures. Imagine if the enemy had got to know about what went on here – it would have made this place top of their list of targets!"

I shifted from one foot to the other. If the corrupt members of staff knew we were on the trail to Dad's evidence, we'd be top of *their* list of targets! We had to get on! Find the lion eagle!

"Say there was a city that they thought might get bombed." Josh paused, and I guessed he must be thinking about my hunch that Lily's dad had worked in Coventry. "Couldn't the people that lived there leave, just in case?"

"What – *might* get bombed? Down tools on a bit of hearsay?" said Percy. "Anywhere *might* get bombed. There was a war on, remember!"

I stared into the Enigma Machine case, wondering if I should just ask Percy about the lion eagle after all. I stared at the weird sort of typewriter through the glass. At least it looked like an old typewriter, except it had two keyboards and some extra dials, and wires that plugged into little holes at the front. There were three windows by the dials that had capital letters in them.

"There are three rotors inside," Percy was saying. "That's why there's three dials."

"The dials change the letters in the windows!" said Josh. You could see he was itching to get his hands on it, and would have done, if there wasn't a box of thick glass all round it.

"You had to set the three letters right first, before you could do anything," Percy said. "It was like a password, you might say, to start things off. The *key*, it was called. . ."

Sasha nudged me with her elbow. "Three letters!" she hissed. "Like the lists in Lily's notebook."

I nodded. The keys for decoding Enigma messages, were they? It still didn't make much sense.

"Now, there would originally have been five rotating dial wheels to choose from," Percy went on. "That's sixty possible ways to set those for starters, and then there are plugs at the front that can be slotted in different positions. . ."

Josh was hanging on his every word.

Sasha pulled me to the side. "OK," she whispered. "This might help us with the Lily story, but what about the lion eagle clue?"

"So how does the electromechanical rotor work exactly?" we heard Josh say to Percy.

I turned back to Sasha. "Just what I was thinking," I said anxiously. I checked my watch. I tried to catch Josh's attention but he was in full swing.

"*The keys were changed at midnight every single day by the enemy,*" he read out loud from a display on the wall, "*so the race was always on at Bletchley to find the day's key.* Did they break all the codes, then?"

"Most of the codes *did* get broken," said Percy. "But if they couldn't get the key for a certain day, the code was called a dead duck and none of the messages could be solved. . ."

"Oh no!" gasped Josh.

"That's the way it was sometimes, though," continued Percy. "Rarely, but sometimes. But they were a determined bunch here at BP! They wouldn't give up easily. Kept hopeful, they did. Where would we be without hope?"

"Do you know anything about someone called Lily Kenley?"

Josh clamped his hand over his mouth as soon as he'd said it. He looked terrified and Sasha scowled at him.

"Sorry," he muttered to me through one side of his mouth.

But I guess I was too worried about Monday to be that cross with him. Too worried about time ticking away and us getting nowhere. And I did want to know about Lily. Maybe knowing more about her would help us with her clue. We had nothing else to go on.

"Kenley?" Percy frowned. "The name rings a bell. . ."

"It's for a *school project*," Josh said earnestly, and I had to give him a little smile to stop him looking so worried.

"Give me a minute. It's coming back to me." Percy tapped his forehead. "We've heard about a Lilian Kenley.

Quite infamous, she was. Thorn in the side of the place. She could have blown everything."

We stared at one another. "What do you mean?" said Sasha.

"Like to keep her quiet, we do," whispered Percy, doing the drama thing again and tapping his nose. "Unofficial, like. Even after all this time! Follow me."

He led us back up the stairs and outside and we crunched along the snowy road and into Hut 8, which we'd passed before.

"Bit warmer in here," said Percy, wiping his shoes on the mat.

We went down a long corridor with all these little rooms to the sides with displays in. I kept my eyes peeled all the way, hoping something would jump out to help me with Lily's clue. I glimpsed a stuffed pigeon peeping out from a capsule under a little parachute . . . the cluttered little office where Alan Turing had worked. . .

There was a room right at the very end of the hut, and a display board in the far corner, and round the back of the board there were laminated sheets of text stuck in a line with drawing pins. "There you go," said Percy. "I knew it was here somewhere. Some info for you there. Don't know what happened to the last card, though."

He looked around the floor and you could tell he was annoyed with the lack of organization. "Must have dropped off. Or someone was messing. I'll have to see to that."

Me and Sasha and Josh crowded round the board and I felt my eyes go wide. *BP's Terrible Secret*, said the title on the first laminated sheet. *The Traitor of Hut 6*. There was a black and white photo by the text, and it was small and blurry, but it was definitely the same woman in the photo back home, definitely Lily, or Lilian, or whoever she was. I started to read fast. *Accused of stealing an Enigma Machine, and found with top-secret papers, Miss Lilian Kenley was arrested in December, 1940, and imprisoned awaiting trial...*

"Nathan!" Sasha gasped as she read it too, and I felt Josh grip my shoulder.

Her story's like your dad's, a voice whispered in my head.

Mum's words came back to me. *One morning Lily was gone.*

I carried on reading.

...Stunned colleagues described Kenley as a quiet, hard-working woman who often volunteered extra shifts, which her superiors later forbade at risk of exhaustion and mistakes. Her landlady, Ethel Vane...

Ethel Vane! Auntie Hilda's mum!

...described her as seldom in the house the days before her arrest, her whereabouts not known.

The Enigma Machine was never recovered. It was assumed it had been returned to the enemy, although she would never say what happened to it. She refused, in fact, to speak at all. After her arrest...

That's where the text ran out.

"Strange, though," commented Percy, studying the cards. "If it was lots of money she was after, why not just tell the Nazis about BP so they could come and bomb it to the ground?" He shrugged. "Still all a bit of a mystery, that whole business, and not something we want to draw too much attention to, you can understand. A security breach on that scale would be extremely damaging for the reputation. . ."

There was the noise of kids running about and loud laughing, and we saw a flash of green uniforms at the other end of the room.

"So what happened to her?" I asked over the din, the question catching in my throat.

"Eh?" Percy was looking at the kids, his eyes like a radar. "Excuse me, would you?"

"Wait! Percy!" I had to know what happened to Lily, but Percy was off, homing in on the rowdy kids like a sheepdog or something.

We hung around a bit, but he didn't appear, so we made our way back through the hut, checking the displays in the little side rooms, and we were just about to give up and go somewhere else when a small board caught my eye. *The truth behind the myth*, the title said. *Bletchley Park and the Coventry Blitz.*

I called to the others, "Look at this," and we huddled together as I read it out.

It talked about how Bletchley Park knew the Moonlight

Sonata raid was coming; how they'd been working round the clock trying to find out which city was the target. . .

I was about to read on when a voice came from beside us. "That's a very controversial story." I flinched sideways.

A woman was standing next to us. She pushed some blonde curls under her black hat, which was speckled with silver sequins, and her feathery earrings swayed about. She laughed, a tinkling kind of laugh. "Some people *still* think that Churchill knew the target was Coventry but pretended not to, although I expect Percy would put them straight about that!"

I looked at her. The long sheepskin coat and black Wellington boots. She didn't look like a corrupt member of staff any more than Percy did, but still. "You know something about the Coventry Blitz?" I asked, keeping my guard up.

She gave me a warm smile. "Bits and pieces. I'm studying for my history PhD." You could see Josh was impressed. She tossed her lime green scarf over one shoulder. "I'm Rose, by the way. Hello."

She tapped the display board gently with the tip of a bright pink umbrella. "Shame the information's so limited." She adjusted the poppy pinned on her coat and clicked the top button of her jacket ready to leave, then looked at us sideways. "You're keen historians, are you?"

"When it's for a school project," Josh said earnestly.

Rose laughed a friendly laugh. "Well, let me think. There'd probably be more information in the archives room. I'm a bit pressed for time, but . . . I could take you there if you like?"

We all trooped off, making trails across the snow. Sasha wasn't saying much, but I felt a fizz of excitement. The archives room – there was bound to be loads of useful stuff in there! Maybe, just maybe, there could be what we needed to solve the lion eagle clue.

We got to the door of the archives building and Rose grinned. "Best not let that Percy see us in here – he'll only be jealous!" She had a special pass in a flip-out plastic wallet with an emblem of an anchor or something on it, and the woman on the front desk shifted up her glasses when she saw it and waved us straight through.

Rose smiled at us and we walked down a very long corridor that seemed to go on for ever.

We stopped at a door and she stamped the melting snow from her boots and slipped them off. "Welcome to my office!" she said, waving us in. "Not bad, is it? Yeah, I come in here quite a lot. Have to even do the night shift sometimes. I've this crazy deadline!"

I knew that feeling.

Rose opened and closed a few drawers and took out a packet of custard creams. "Grab a few of those," she said, dumping them on the desk. She sunk her teeth into a biscuit and started opening filing cabinets, then slamming them shut.

"Are you sure this is a good idea, Nathan?" Sasha said to

me out of the corner of her mouth. "How do we know we can trust her?"

"She seems OK," I said. "A bit weird, maybe. But we haven't exactly told her much."

Josh chomped the top off a custard cream and Sasha pulled a face at me.

Rose wrenched open a drawer and started rifling through it. "I love research! Bit of a treasure hunt, isn't it? Let's see."

Sasha fidgeted in her seat, then looked at me, frowning and tapping her watch with a finger. She was right. I looked at the rows and rows of metal filing cabinets, and the shelves going up to the ceiling. Where would you even start in a place like this? My hopes about the archives room started fading fast. This was all taking way too long.

Rose slammed one drawer shut and opened another.

"Where's the Coventry Blitz information, then?" Sasha asked impatiently.

"Ah, top secret and classified, that is," Rose said. "I can tell you, but I'd have to kill you afterwards!"

We all laughed. All except Sasha.

"Thing is, Rose," said Sasha, out of patience, "we have to go soon, so if you can just show us the stuff about Coventry, please."

"Course!" she cooed. Rose waggled a couple of files from the drawers and slapped them down on the table. "You have a look at that, Sash, and there's one for you, Joshua my lad. One's about the Blitz and the other has copies of all the displays in Bletchley!"

Josh beamed and started looking through a chunky file with a thick elastic band round it, stamped:

COVENTRY BLITZ:
THE MOONLIGHT SONATA RAID

Rose's mobile phone rang. She flashed us an apologetic smile and padded out of the room in her socks to answer it.

"*Nathan!*" Sasha hissed. "Why are we wasting so much time here?"

"We're trying to find out what lion eagle means!" I whispered back. "Don't you want to know?"

"Course I do," grumped Sasha. Her shoulders twitched. "Pass me that silly file, then!" I shoved over *Master copies of displayed texts* and she opened up the cover. "Let's get to work! Anything *lion eagle*."

Rose came back looking hassled. "PhD supervisors!" she said, pulling her boots from under the table. "I've got to shoot off. Get back to uni. Listen, I had a word with the lady on the desk and you can stay longer in here if you want." She wagged a finger at us. "No touching anything else, though, OK?" she said firmly, giving us a look. Then she fluttered her fingers in a wave and left.

I jumped up and rushed out after her. "Rose, I just wanted to ask you. . ."

But the long corridor was empty. Funny. She moved fast. I went back in and closed the door.

Sasha slapped over a page of her file. "I thought we weren't supposed to be trusting anyone, Nathan! But first Percy, now this Rose woman!" She stood up and went over to a filing cabinet and opened a drawer.

"What are you *doing*?" said Josh, pulling on the strings of his hood with alarm. "Rose said we couldn't. . ."

"Shhh!" Sasha shut the drawer with a bang. Then she went round the back of Josh, whipped the Coventry file from off the table and shoved it under her coat.

"You can't!" protested Josh.

"I just did!" Sasha's face was flushed, triumphant. "Besides, I'm just borrowing it. There's way too much in there to read now. I'll give it back."

She sat down again and turned the pages of *Master copies of displayed texts* huffily. "Seriously, though, it could be useful, right, Nathan? You told us you think Lily's dad was living in Coventry, and that Lily was trying to find out if that was the target of the raid. Or do you prefer to ask Rose all about it?"

"But she can't just take it, Nathan," Josh fretted. "They might notice it's missing. They might know it was us and. . ."

"Nathan." Sasha pulled out a page from her file and touched my shoulder lightly. All the moodiness had gone out of her voice. "I found it. A copy of that missing card. From that display board about Lily."

"What?" I lurched up. "Let me see."

She fingered one corner of the sheet, bending it. "Are you sure you want to know?"

"Yes." My mouth felt all dry like feathers. I did want to know, course I did, but. . . That stuff about her in prison, about her being charged with stealing secrets. . .

"Maybe you shouldn't look," said Sasha, holding the card away from me. "It's not good news."

I stood up. "*Please*, Sash!"

She sighed, then handed the card over, and I started to read.

. . .*Kenley died in prison after only a few days*. . . I stopped and let out a gasp. I read on, the other words coming in snatches . . . *weak heart* . . . *despite efforts to resuscitate her*. . . I saw Dad, an old man on the floor of a cell. . . *Always known as the Traitor of Bletchley Park*. . . *Traitor*. . .

The newspaper headline banged into my head. TRAITOR! TRAITOR! The jeering kids in the street. Then I couldn't read any more. I held on to the edge of the table.

And then Sasha and Josh were either side of me, familiar voices from far away, calling out my name.

10

Lion Eagle

"**N**athan!" Sasha pushed a steaming cup across the table.

We were in the Bletchley Park café by the lake, huddled by the window.

I didn't have time for stupid hot chocolate! We had to get on with the trail; work out what lion eagle meant. Sasha must have seen how impatient I was.

"Just a quick break," she said. "To plan our next move."

"You've had a nasty shock," said Josh, tucking into the plate of cakes Sasha had ordered. "You need sugar."

I sat up a little, gazing at the murk outside through the speckles of melting snow on the glass. Was that a figure standing watching by the lake? I squinted at the water's edge again, but there was no one.

I picked at the icing on a vanilla slice with my finger.

"They're going to charge my dad," I said numbly.

"*What?*"

I told them about Dad's transfer.

"Monday?" repeated Sasha. "Oh Nathan, *no!*"

"I saw a film once where someone was charged with breaking the terrorism laws," said Josh, "and it was really bad because. . ." He stopped and fiddled with his stuck-up hair. "Well, we need our combined brainpower if we're going to solve the trail in time." He turned to Sasha. "What about that file you pinched?"

"I didn't pinch it, OK?" said Sasha, all bossy and flustered. "I'm not getting it out in *here*." She ripped a white sachet open and tipped the sugar in her drink, stirring it hard, and Josh went quiet and bit into a slice of jam sponge.

An old couple came into the café and sat down. The café woman came to take away an old cup and smiled at us as she gave our table a quick wipe. A telly fixed on the wall droned in the background and a weatherman swept an arm across a big map of Britain. "*A band of snow will be moving across the country over the next few days . . . unusual weather for this time of year. . . Only essential journeys are recommended in. . .*"

I braced myself, expected to see a story about Leon Vane the Traitor any minute, but none came. I swigged the syrupy leftovers of my lukewarm chocolate.

Was Dad innocent? A terrible doubt niggled me, and I was ashamed for even thinking it. Dad *was* innocent, I told myself. He'd told me he was. I trusted him. I trusted him more than anyone.

Twirling snowflakes caught on the café window and stayed there. I pressed my face against the cold glass as the drive got whiter. People hurried away under their umbrellas. The snow fell faster. Strange yellow clouds cast lemon-white light, and the ground was feathery and full of shadows, like night was almost here.

My phone buzzed and I fished it out of my pocket and looked at the screen with its ghost-green letters.

07700900583

This is Lily. Help me Nath. . .

Right then I could have half-believed it really *was* Lily sending me a message. Lily back from the grave. Lily wanting me to clear her name.

I lowered my voice. "Lily texted me," I said. "Twice."

Josh and Sasha looked at me like I was delirious.

"I don't really think it was her, do I?" I showed them the texts on my phone.

Sasha gasped, and Josh put his cake down very slowly, missing his plate and smearing jam on the menu.

"I'm sorry, Nathan," said Josh, tugging an edge of tablecloth. "It's probably my fault. When I said those things about Lily. . ."

"Forget it," I said. "I should have told you about the texts sooner. I guess I didn't want to scare you."

"But I'm already scared," said Josh. "Very scared. Don't use your phone again!" he pleaded, rubbing his hands together over and over. "The corrupt staff could have hacked into it! Whatever you do, don't text back either. Don't use your phone for *anything*! Definitely no texts and definitely no talking!"

"Josh's right, Nathan," said Sasha. "Be really careful."

I nodded grimly and watched Josh cleaning the menu with his sleeve.

Then I grabbed it off him and stared at the top of the front cover. It was the photo I was interested in. It was a shot of the main door of the mansion. . . I stared and stared at the photo, and then, despite everything, I started laughing. I couldn't help it.

"What is it, Nathan?" Sasha and Josh probably thought I'd gone mental. I pointed and waited while the penny dropped. Josh looked at the photo, wide-eyed, then chuckled.

Sasha jumped out of her chair and sprang up and down with excitement, making the old couple stare. "The griffins, Nathan," she whispered. "The griffin statues either side of the mansion door! They're half eagle and half lion!"

Sasha turned to me, her eyes shining. "Your dad *knew* you'd work it out, Nathan. He believed in you, and we do too." She gave my hand a squeeze, and Josh nodded.

"Excellent!" he laughed, cramming cake in his mouth and stuffing the rest in his pockets as we pulled on our coats and made for the door.

11

The Old Griffins

We didn't have far to go. The mansion was right next door.

The two stone griffins stood there, paws raised and frowning, as if they'd been waiting for us and were wondering what had taken us so long. If the workmen hadn't been in the way, or that group of schoolkids. . .

I peered around to check nobody was about, then started to look over the griffin on the left, while Sasha and Josh went for the one on the right. I ran my fingers over its smooth white wings and brushed the ice off its beak, looking for a carving, a message, anything. Maybe a secret opening with something shoved inside.

The griffin still looked so clean after so many years, so new. *Don't panic*, I told myself. I searched the surface of the statue, checking the grooves on the feathered neck and paws, pressing my fingertips in the ears and the clefts around its eyes.

"I'm sorry to say this, Nathan," said Josh after a few minutes, "but they don't look very nineteen forties."

I knelt there on the icy ground, searching all around the base. *Stop fooling yourself*, I told myself. It was obvious these were new statues, not decades old. They couldn't possibly be any part of Lily's trail.

My hands went slack. The snow turned to sleet and an icy wind blew it into our faces. We pulled up our hoods. Wafts of music sounded from inside the house, that same ballroom tune, over and over, doing my head in. Somewhere nearby was the sound of a running engine. A few people scuttled past us to get inside the house. The lake lay there like grey glass.

A woman with an umbrella walked quickly past. The same lady who'd served us in the café.

"Excuse me!" I shouted after her. "Wait!"

She swivelled towards us, her face pinched up with cold.

"The griffins," I called. "Are they new?"

She gave us a quick nod. "Big improvement on the others, if you ask me," she said, battling with her umbrella.

My heartbeat speeded up. "What do you mean?"

"The old griffins." She pulled her collar up around her neck. "In a terrible condition, they were."

She turned to go, but I fired another question. "What happened to them?"

I dreaded her answer. They might be long gone, destroyed, along with any chance to save Dad.

"They're somewhere in the old storeroom," the woman said, "last time I knew. Next to Hut 11? Yes, Hut 11, I think." Then she hurried away.

Sasha already had the map out and we scanned it. Josh pointed a finger. "That way!" he said, and we were off.

We got to Hut 11. It had a run-down room next to it, an open-sided brick thing with a corrugated roof and a barrier of hexagonal chicken wire along the front. The brick side had a splintering wooden door with a padlock and a slightly open little window high up one wall. It was dingy inside and hard to make things out. It had all these bits of old stuff in there – a bike with a basket propped against one wall, planks leaned up against each other, and all kinds of metal pieces and coils of rope.

But in the far corner. . .

I put my face to the wire and squinted to make out the shapes. . .

Two old griffin statues, huddled together in the shadows.

"That's them!" confirmed Sasha. She rattled the padlock on the door, then pulled at the chicken wire, but it wouldn't budge. "How do we get in?"

"We're going to have to do breaking and entering!" said Josh, looking scared. "I'm the thinnest." He stretched up towards the little window. "Maybe I could get through there if I breathed right in. Give me a lift up, Nathan," he said, clawing at the wall.

"Hang on!" I really didn't like the idea of him going up,

but what choice was there? I glanced around. The place was deserted. I crouched to the ground. "Climb up then, Josh."

I stood there with him wobbling on my shoulders. He was a lot heavier than he looked, a dead weight; must have been all those cakes. My back and neck were killing me. "Nearly!" called Josh. "Just a bit higher!"

"It's a lot easier with keys, young men."

I felt Josh grip my head and it took all my strength to stop him toppling sideways. I stooped to let him slide off and stood up straight with a groan.

Percy stood there, arms folded. He was trying to look severe, but I saw a little smile on his lips. He took out a big bunch of keys. "If it isn't our Josh and friends. More research? No homes to go to? What's taken your interest in here, then?"

We stood there, staring at him like idiots. Percy looked for the right key, waggling them one by one in the lock. "Awful state a lot of the Bletchley buildings were in," he said. "Still are. National disgrace, if you ask me. There was even talk of knocking the whole place down, would you believe? We soon put a stop to that, thanks to our campaigning." He searched through the bunch and stabbed in another key. "The work here shortened the war by two years, they say. National disgrace to even *think* about getting rid of it."

"Yes, Rose was telling me something about that," said Josh. "On the way to the archive room."

"Eh?" said Percy. "Who? There we go!" The padlock snapped open and he pushed open the door.

"Probably getting – you know – forgetful," Josh whispered, but Sasha just raised her eyebrows at me.

"Distract Percy while I check the griffins," I muttered.

I wandered away while Sash and Josh pretended to be really interested in the old bike and asked Percy loads of questions about its brake system and tyre pressure, and Josh actually sounded like he really *was* interested.

I crouched by the old griffins, running my hands over their mottled grey stone feathers. They were so different to the ones by the mansion door. Their features were almost worn away. They smiled at me sadly with their crumbling mouths and I thought they looked more like decayed angels than griffins.

"Closing time soon, kids," I heard Percy say. "We're shutting up earlier today, on account of the snow clogging up the roads."

I winced. I'd thought we had longer.

"You should be getting home, and me too," went on Percy. "I've done my shift for today and my missus will have the tea on. Likes me to be on time, she does. There's trouble if I'm not!"

I scanned the pitted stone, the rough scraggy wings. There had to be something! Hurry! I twisted my head to look. Then, on the back of the neck, I found a neat little engraving of a full moon with a crescent shape inside with lines coming from it.

I checked the other griffin. It had the same thing, only. . .

I couldn't believe it!

On *this* griffin there were extra lines, scratched hard in the stone.

The lines made the central moonbeam into an arrow, and at the end of the arrow . . . I rubbed my fingers over the marks . . . a star had been gouged, a four-pointed star with wonky lines, like it had been done in a great big hurry.

The next clue! It had to be. Lily's next clue! I didn't have a pen and paper, but I had to record the picture somehow. I remembered the camera on my phone and without thinking I pulled it out and took a picture with that, the flash filling the space with light.

Too late, I remembered what Josh had said about my phone being hacked.

"Taking pictures as well now, are you?" smiled Percy, heading for the door, steering us in front of him. "All very Secret Service! I really do need to be going, though, kids. All out now, please – that's the ticket! No doubt we'll meet again."

We watched Percy hurry through a side gate in the chain-link fence, pull it shut behind him and disappear off.

"Please don't tell me you used your phone," said Josh, hopping from foot to foot as I held out the screen for them to see.

So stupid! "It's too late to worry," I said, all worried. "Just look."

They peered at the fuzzy photo. "He found the next clue, Josh!" cried Sasha, dancing a bit in the snow. "Nathan found it!"

"Any ideas, though?" I said.

Josh scratched his head. "A moonbeam pointing to a star? Nothing comes to mind just yet."

That's when I saw the bunch of keys still hanging from the storeroom padlock. I took a quick look around and then I shoved them in my pocket.

"You can't!" said Josh, horrified. "They're Percy's!"

"They could be useful," I said, trying to convince myself that what I was doing wasn't all that terrible. "Say we need to get back inside this shed and take another look at the griffin." I looked at Sasha and she gave a small shrug.

"You're just *borrowing* them," she said. "You'll give them back."

"Closing time, kids."

We spun round to see a man standing there, the same security guard we'd seen on our way in. Had he seen me grab the keys? I thought in a panic.

"I'll escort you to the gate," he said. He still wasn't smiling. He wasn't just asking either.

We followed him back the way we'd come, and he stood watching us as we trooped out past the car park, and that's when we saw the car.

It was in amongst the other parked cars, and it had tinted windows. I caught my breath. The driver's window was slightly down, but we couldn't see in. The glass slid closed and the car pulled away.

"Do you think that was them?" gabbled Josh. "The same people sending the texts? The ones trying to frame your dad?"

"Let's get home," whispered Sasha, pulling at my arm.

"They're just trying to scare us off," I said, my voice shaky. "Just act normal."

Josh fumbled a serviette parcel from his pocket and took out a mangled chocolate éclair, nearly dropping it. "Beethoven, by the way," he said nervously as we set off, his cheeks full up like a hamster.

"What?" I walked along, trying not to hurry, trying to look normal. What had Josh said?

"That music they were playing in the ballroom," he munched. "Der, der, der. Der, der, der. Der, der, der. Der, der, der. It came to me. It's by Beethoven. Ludwig van Beethoven." Josh ate a last fragment of éclair and wiped the cream from his mouth with his sleeve as we headed for the bus stop.

"It's the music of the *Moonlight Sonata*."

12
Moonlight Sonata

*D*ad is at the piano in the front room, playing the *same notes over and over, a ball and chain tied round one ankle. I'm outside, looking in through the big bay window.*

Big logs blaze in the fireplace and there are noises overhead, like planes doing low passes over the house, but when I look up the sky is pitch back and I don't see a thing. I press my nose against the cold glass. There's a dropped cigarette on the rug in front of the fire, sending up coils of smoke.

I shout. Tap on the window.

Dad carries on playing. He has a mask on now, a grinning mask like the guy on the bonfire, and now there is a ring of flames dancing around the cigarette stub.

I tap harder.

The sound of planes gets louder, but I still can't see anything.

A snake of fire slips across the carpet. The curtains catch light. I bang on the glass and it's warm under my palm and I'm yelling, screaming for Dad to stop, to get out. But he carries on sitting there, playing the piano, smoke thick around him. Not hearing. Not listening. And right above me is the wailing of bombs being dropped. Bombs falling through the air until the screeching hurts my ears.

Someone stumbles behind me, grips my arm. I spin round and there is Lily, her hair all messed up, her eyes wild, her mouth wide. "Help me, Nat!" she screams. "I have to save my dad. I have to break the Enigma. I have to save my. . ."

DAD!

My eyes snapped open and I sat up. My bedroom was deadly quiet and a yellowish light was coming through my curtains. The fabric moved from some invisible draught. The pane was powdered with snow. I pulled the duvet round me, shivering, letting my bad dream sink away.

There was the smell of bacon cooking and it dawned on me that it was my birthday. The thirteenth of November. Sunday. I was thirteen now. Mum must be making me my birthday breakfast.

I didn't want it to be my birthday – there were too many other things to think about, like solving the trail before tomorrow. The crescent and the arrow pointing to a star. Saving Dad.

But I might get to speak to him today, I remembered

with a jolt. Mr Edwards had semi-promised, hadn't he? But what would I say? What *could* I say, when anyone might be listening in?

What time was it? I fumbled to check on my watch, then groaned. Nearly half ten! How could I have slept in and wasted precious time like that?

I fumbled with my mobile. I was supposed to phone Sasha and Josh as soon as I woke up, just let the phone ring three times so they'd know to come round so we could carry on trying to work out the clue – definitely no texts and definitely no talking. I did the ringing, then groaned again. Half a whole morning of working out the moon and star drawing was gone for good.

Deadline. Dead end.

Music started thumping through the wall from Hannah's room. My pillow was all lumpy and I pulled out the chunky file from under it.

COVENTRY BLITZ:
THE MOONLIGHT SONATA RAID

Might we have missed something in it last night? Might there be something to help with the drawing on the griffin after all? I pulled off the elastic band and turned the pages fast.

November fourteenth. That weird coincidence. Dad getting charged. Had that been Lily's deadline as well, to break Enigma codes and save her dad? Her story had really got to me, the way it was somehow wound up tight inside my dad's. Lily in prison, branded a traitor – me trying to stop that happening to him.

There was the newspaper clipping with a couple of black and white photos, the smoking shell of a cathedral with its roof gone; a street full of rubble and caved-in houses with the caption underneath: *Last night came the worst bombing Coventry has ever seen*. The photo of barrage balloons flying over the city, and a big anti-aircraft gun pointing at the sky.

I thought about Coventry burning, Lily's dad, the hunch I had that he'd lived there. If I could just find that out for sure. It might somehow lead me to the breakthrough I needed with Lily's trail.

It came to me suddenly. The old address book! The one with the red velvety cover in the hall cabinet. The guest book had dated right back – the address book might too. And if Lily had stayed in the house a while, her home address might be in there as well, mightn't it?

I scrambled out of bed, pulled on some clothes and slipped downstairs. From the kitchen came the sounds of cutlery banging together; the smells of mushrooms cooked in butter, of bacon getting crispier.

I went into the hall. **TELL NOBODY** said the poster sternly as I pulled open the drawer and took the book out. It felt weird, thinking everyone in it was probably dead. A list of dead people, in tidy alphabetical order. I leafed quickly through to "K".

Lily Elizabeth Kenley

And underneath. . . My skin prickled. I couldn't believe it. There it was.

13 Cathedral Street, Coventry

And something else.

Next of kin: Albert James Kenley (Father)

(See address above.)

I gripped the book. Lily's dad *was* living in Coventry – this proved it! The only family she had left. Bletchley knew a huge raid was coming, and Lily must have known too.

Why didn't Lily just phone him up, then – plead with her dad to leave the city just in case? Percy's voice rattled through my head. *What – down tools on a bit of hearsay? There was a war on!*

No, Lily had to find out whether Coventry was definitely the target or not. Was *that* why she'd stolen the Enigma Machine, why she'd been found with secret papers? Not a traitor at all, just someone trying to save her dad. My throat went tight. The same way I was trying to save mine.

Had my dad known all this stuff, I wondered, or had he just found and followed Lily's trail, not knowing her real story?

I looked impatiently at my watch. When would Sasha and Josh get here? I had to tell them what I'd found out. Knowing more about Lily might give us a lead for the griffin clue. Did she break the codes in time? The question

144

echoed round my head: *Did she save her dad?*

I remembered another photo from the Coventry file: one of a man in a tin hat with a fire hose in front of a massive blaze. Mum's words came back: *Lily's dad was posted as a fireman or something.*

I fingered the address book again.

A list of the dead.

A thought shot through me.

What about the Internet? That could have a list of all the Coventry victims.

I went into the front room and edged open a corner of curtain. The drive was white with snow. I looked up and down the empty lane.

I got out my laptop and started it up. I typed *coventry blitz victims* into Google and my fingers felt clammy as I slid them over the touch pad, clicking on what I needed.

There were lots of names, too many names, like the long lists of soldiers on our village war memorial. I scrolled down until I got to the one name I'd dreaded finding there.

Kenley, Albert James

I sat there, all numb and floating, like I wasn't properly in my body any more.

Fire warden. Died while saving others from a collapsing house.

It was like something inside me came crashing down. Lily hadn't cracked the code. She hadn't saved her dad.

What if I couldn't crack the code? What if I couldn't save mine?

I looked at the piano stool with its lion's feet made of dark, polished wood, its padded velvet seat, all wrinkled and buckled. I remembered what Auntie Hilda had told Mum, about Lily sitting there, playing the same piece over and over.

Cobwebs crackled as I lifted the piano seat and sifted through the dusty music books. It was near the bottom of the pile, all battered with its spine hanging off.

MOONLIGHT SONATA
BY
LUDWIG VAN BEETHOVEN

I think I'd already expected it when I found Lily's name pencilled in the front. This was the piece she'd played, over and over, as if she somehow hoped the music would help her break the codes.

"Morning, love."

Mum came up behind me and gave me a hug. She smelled of cooking bacon, and flowers from the special perfume Dad bought her last Christmas, and I stayed there, breathing her in.

She was smiling, but her face looked pale and tired. I was worried she'd ask me about the piano book, but she didn't even look at it.

"I thought the smell of a full English would get you out of bed! Happy birthday, love."

I didn't want it to be my birthday. I didn't want to have to be happy. I wanted Sasha and Josh to get here and I wanted to solve the moon and star clue as fast as possible! And I wanted to know what to say to Dad if he phoned! But I said thanks and gave her a smile back and tried to pretend.

Hannah came down dressed in black leggings and a long black pullover that went past her knees. "Happy birthday," she said, tossing a perfectly wrapped round present the exact size of a football that bounced before I caught it. "Will keep you guessing for days, baby brother."

I pulled off the coloured paper. It was a football, but not just any old football. I held it in two hands. It was one signed by all the England team, black leather pentagons with a name in black pen on each white hexagon. They weren't cheap. Josh and I had seen one in the posh sports shop in town. Hannah had probably spent a lot more than one Saturday's wages on it.

I wanted to hug her and say it was the best present I'd ever had, but I just stood there staring at the football like an idiot. "Thanks," I managed to say at last. "It's . . . it's really nice."

We'll have a kick-around later, Nat, Dad said in my head.

Hannah shrugged and shoved her headphones in her ears.

"This is from Dad." Mum went to the Welsh dresser and got out the thick silver envelope I'd seen hidden there. "He wrote the card a few days ago, before. . ." Mum's voice trailed off.

I stared at the front of the envelope, at the Happy Birthday, Nat and the way the silver paper flashed all the rainbow colours in the light. I peeled it open as slowly as I could and eased the card out. It was one of those ones you make yourself, with cut corners for slipping a photo in, and Dad had put a photo of the four of us, sitting together laughing. I looked at what he'd written inside.

To my dearest NAT,
The very best son any DAD could HOPE for.
With all my LOVE for ALWAYS and ever,
Dad XXX

NAT DAD HOPE LOVE ALWAYS. I held the edges of the card tight.

I thought about people listening in like we were here as entertainment. My skin crawled and went hot. I imagined them sitting with their feet up, with their headphones and their extra large tubs of popcorn, waiting for my phone call with Dad, waiting for me to slip up. If only I could ask him about the drawing on the griffin! If only he could tell me straight where the trail was leading!

I pushed Dad's card inside the front pocket of my fleece and closed the zip tight.

"See what else is in the envelope then," said Mum, her voice catching.

I slipped my fingers back inside the silver envelope and pulled out two tickets. Football tickets for the semi-final match next Saturday. Special box seats. Two tickets; one for me and one for Dad. I felt them tremble between my fingers. Next Saturday seemed a lifetime away.

"This is from me." Mum quickly pushed another present into my hand and I pulled at the wrapping, glad to have something to rip apart and screw up. Socks, chocolate, some gift vouchers for the game shop. "Not very imaginative, I'm afraid. Right!" she said brightly, digging a hanky from her yellow work bag hanging from the chair and quickly dabbing her eyes with it. "I'd better check the eggs and bacon. As your dad would say, there's nothing like the sound of bubbling fat!"

Nothing like the sound of bubbling fat, eh, Nat?

Me and Hannah sat in silence, me racking my brains over the clue, her texting on her phone. The arrow along the moonbeam . . . pointing to a star. . .

"Set the table!" Mum called round the kitchen door, launching a tablecloth at me.

Hannah sat by the fire, dumping on wood and prodding the flames while I cleared the front room table of junk and smoothed the cloth over it. I set out the cutlery and the plates and the salt and vinegar and the ketchup bottle, and the bottle of brown sauce that only Dad liked. Then I realized I'd laid a place for Dad without thinking and I was about to take the extras away but I saw Hannah watching me from where she was crouched by the fire and she shook her head slightly and said, "Leave them there, Nathan."

Mum came out of the kitchen carrying a stack of serving dishes between a pair of oven gloves, smiling her too-bright smile.

"Heck, Mother," said Hannah. "You're even wearing lipstick!"

"I thought we should celebrate Nathan's birthday properly," said Mum, blowing her fringe out of her face and glancing at the extra place. She dumped the serving dishes on the table and went back to get more stuff.

There were runny fried eggs and scrambled eggs and mushrooms with black pepper and baked beans and crispy fried bread, and thick sausages with their sides splitting, and big glasses of orange juice with bits in, and fried tomatoes with their seeds spilling out.

"Does it look all right?" Mum asked as she sat down.

I managed a smile. Mum was trying so hard, I wanted to hug her. But the last thing I wanted to do was sit and have brunch.

We started to eat, listening to Mum talking about her hospital ward, and the number of extra broken bones there'd been in the icy weather, and how she'd have to go into work for a Sunday shift later, and about the rising price of petrol. . . Anything, so long as it wasn't about Dad.

150

I looked at the empty place again. Did all this feel right without him? The bacon suddenly wasn't quite as tasty as it had seemed at the start. I saw Hannah picking at her plate, the food only half-finished. I struggled to get the mouthfuls down.

Mum got seconds from the kitchen and started piling it on our plates. A ridiculous number of sausages, big dollops of mushrooms. Hannah waved a hand over her plate. "Ease off, Mother! These leggings have a limit to how much they can stretch."

Mum sat back down with the serving spoon, turning her wedding ring round and round. She stared at the wall where three bright blue butterflies were pinned inside a glass frame. Our fire spat and smoked, feeble. Dad would have had the fire roaring up the chimney in no time.

The phone rang, breaking the tension and then pulling it tight. I nearly choked on my orange juice. Mum leapt up and answered and stood by the door with the receiver. "Mr Edwards? Hello. . . Yes. . . You're joking? Really? How did you manage to get them to agree to that? *Really?* But just Nathan? I understand."

She held the phone out to me, her eyes shining. "Nathan, it's your dad!"

Dad. I gaped at her, then scrambled up from my place. Mr Edwards had really managed to sort it. A birthday call from Dad. I felt a smile explode across my face. Then I was suddenly really scared. Scared because the corrupt members of staff would be listening in, scared I'd make a blunder and give the game away. I should have thought this through better first. Practised exactly what to say.

"Don't you want to speak to him first?" I stammered.

Mum took a step towards me with the receiver. "He's only got permission to speak to you." I saw the pain in her face. Hannah's too. But I also saw the way they were looking at me, urging me on, desperate to know how Dad was. "Come on, love."

I took the phone. Mum and Hannah had their eyes fixed on me. "Dad?" I whispered.

"Happy birthday, Nat."

Just hearing his voice sent a shiver through me. All the things I wanted to tell him, but couldn't, churned through my head. *I'm almost at the end of Lily's trail, Dad. They'd moved the griffins, did you know that? But we managed to find the next clue anyway. I don't understand it yet, but I'm working on it. . .*

"How are you?" I struggled.

"I'm fine. Just want to be home. Thirteen at last, Nathan!"

My brain was suddenly on red alert. Dad was calling me Nathan. Dad never called me Nathan.

"Did you like the card? Your mum wrote it."

No she didn't, I thought, *you did*, but Dad's voice was rattling on, like he had to squash loads of words in and there was no space to interrupt him. Like in our conversation by the bonfire. What was he trying to tell me this time?

"I hope the heating's working OK, and by the way, if

your mum needs to fill up the car, tell her to use the petrol from BP, Nathan."

BP? He said BP!

"What do you think of the tickets? The ruddy quarter-final, eh?"

Not quarter-final. Semi-final.

"Take the whole thing when you go to the match, the whole book, Nathan. There's some vouchers for half-time snacks in there and things. Take Josh if I'm not back by then. Or Sasha. You shouldn't waste them. I think it's important that you go there, Nathan. Have I been in the papers?"

The question jarred through me. "Yes," I said quietly and I heard Dad pause. "So the press have the story already," he said more slowly. "Soon they'll have the whole story, Nathan."

I'll get to the end, Dad. Just like I promised. I'll find the evidence.

"Look after your mum, son, and your sister."

"I will." My tongue felt all fat. *I need you, Dad. I love you*, but "Thanks for the birthday card," was the only stupid thing I could think of to say.

"Hope you like the message in the card, Nathan," said Dad. He sounded three kisses down the phone and then there was a click and Mr Edwards was on the other end asking to talk to Mum again, and that was it. Time up.

Dad was gone.

13
Making a Wish

Dad never ever calls me Nathan. My brain buzzed as I thought back through what he'd said, forcing myself to remember every detail. *Thirteen at last, Nathan . . . use the petrol from BP, Nathan . . . use the whole book, Nathan . . . it's important that you go there, Nathan. . .*

Hannah was giving me funny looks, but I ignored her. *Soon they'll have the whole story, Nathan. . .*

Hope you like the message in the card, Nathan. . .

Saying Mum wrote my card when she didn't. Saying it was the ruddy quarter-finals when it was the semis. He'd sworn at me again. And what about those sloppy kisses down the phone? He knew I hated stuff like that. That sealed it. He was definitely, *definitely* talking in code. There must be a hidden message in what he was saying. The question was, what?

Mum carried on talking to Mr Edwards, and I heard

snatches of her conversation from the kitchen. "CCTV footage? . . . What car park? . . . A cash handover?"

"How was he, then?" asked Hannah. "What did he say?"

"Not much," I said. "He had hardly any time."

"But how did he *sound*?" she insisted. "Did he seem OK?"

"Yes," I said. It sounded so bland. "He seemed OK."

Hannah looked at the wall, and then she spoke quietly. "What if he's guilty, Nathan?" she said.

I stared at her. I thought about that gang from school. "Has somebody said something to you?"

Her mouth was a grim line. "Let's just say at times like this, you really do learn who your friends are."

Suddenly I felt so sorry for my sister. She didn't know anything about Lily's trail. If only I could tell her there was hope, make her feel better. It was cruel not involving her.

But that thing she'd said, about Dad being guilty. I felt my face scrunch up like wrapping paper. "Dad can't have done anything wrong!"

"What if he *did*?" Hannah said. Her eyes blazed. "He might not have *meant* to, not at first. But who wouldn't be tempted by the right kind of money? Maybe he did steal files and sell them to the highest bidder!"

Anger and doubt rose up inside me. "My dad wouldn't!" I spat at her. "*Our* dad. He wouldn't do something like that! He's *innocent*!"

"Until proven guilty!" Hannah had her hand up. "Stop talking about it now." Hannah picked up her fork and pressed it into the table. "Don't you dare say a word to Mum about what I said, either, not a word! She's at cracking-up point as it is!"

I sat there biting my lip, trying to think about something else, nothing, anything, so I wouldn't have to think about what Hannah had said; admit to what I'd thought myself.

An ember glowed in the pile of ash in the fireplace and upturned horseshoes glinted from the brickwork. The clock ticked, and the pipes clicked and tapped like someone trying to tell me things in code. Dad and Lily watched me from the mantelpiece, and the carrier pigeon stared with its one glass eye.

Whispers trickled through my head: *What if he is guilty? Guilty. Guilty.* I scowled. "He's innocent," I muttered.

What I had to do was concentrate on Dad's phone call; on what he'd really been trying to tell me.

Thirteen at last, Nathan

The petrol from BP, Nathan

The whole book, Nathan

Important that you go there, Nathan

Could Dad have been trying to help me with Lily's trail? *Why* weren't Sasha and Josh here yet? I thought with frustration. They must have got my three rings!

"Full, kids?" Mum reappeared and gathered up our plates in a hurry, like she was trying to hide the wasted food on them. Both of us waited for her to tell us what Mr Edwards had said, but she just took the plates away and I heard her scraping them into the dog bowl.

"Ta-da!" She came back in carrying a birthday cake, a chunky thing with green icing and plastic footballers running about on it, and *XIII* iced on in big Roman numerals like Dad would have done, and a ring of lit candles.

"But we've only just had a huge Full English!" protested Hannah.

"Just a small piece," said Mum. "Nathan's to make his wish." Mum set the cake down and the three of us stared at it. "Make a wish then, Nathan," said Mum, her voice low and urgent.

We all leaned in around the table and it was like she and Hannah were pressing forward, staring at the flames, willing me on, because we all knew there was only one wish to make, only one wish I could make, and if there was any magic, any scrap of power in that wish. . .

I stared at the circle of little flames, feeling the heat rise up my face. *I wish. . .*

I wish Dad would come home.

I blew the candles out and the smoke spiralled and spread and Mum drew back and nodded, like the ritual had been performed right. She pulled out the candles and jabbed a knife in the middle of the cake, footballers scattering like they'd been in a bomb blast. She eased out two big wedges of cake and dropped them on to plates for Hannah and me.

157

I put some cake in my mouth. It was very sweet. Sickly. I coughed on a crumb, then forced it down, but my face must have given the game away.

"We *are* allowed to enjoy ourselves," Mum said, her voice gone up a pitch. Never a good sign.

"Yes, Mother," said Hannah, stabbing at her cake with a finger. "We are. This is great. Calm down."

The three of us stared at the place where Dad wasn't.

"Your *other cards*, Nathan!" said Mum, suddenly, like she'd just remembered she'd found the Holy Grail. She rushed off to get them and fanned the envelopes out in front of me. There was one from Sasha's mum and dad with a book token in it, one from our relatives up north. . . But I was hardly looking at them. I was thinking about what Dad had said on the phone, the words tumbling over and over:

Thirteen at last, Nathan

The petrol from BP, Nathan

The whole book, Nathan

Important that you go there, Nathan

I passed Mum the birthday cards and she squinted at them. "Find my glasses, will you, Hannah, love?"

I was about to open another card when Hannah came back to the table, shaking a bottle of pills and flapping a leaflet at Mum. "What's this?"

Mum straightened in her chair. "Since when did you have the right to go rifling about in my bag, young lady?"

"You asked me to find your glasses! Now are you going to tell us what this is?"

"A bottle of sleeping pills," said Mum, matter-of-factly. "My doctor prescribed them and. . ."

"*This!*" yelled Hannah, tossing the pill bottle away and slapping down the leaflet. I knew what it was. *HM Prison Service – Support for Families of Long Term Inmates.*

"It's Nathan's birthday, Hannah," said Mum. "Do you think we can discuss this later?"

"No we can't," said Hannah. "I'm sick of all these secrets and you not telling us everything!" Mum tried to yank the leaflet off her but Hannah whipped it away so a big piece of corner ripped off in Mum's hand.

"What's going on?" I said. Hannah had obviously totally forgotten what she'd said earlier about not upsetting Mum. I didn't have time for all this pointless arguing.

"It's just something Mr Edwards gave me," Mum began.

Hannah gave a hysterical laugh. "Oh, so Dad's solicitor thinks he's going to prison for the long term now, does he? That's reassuring!"

"He doesn't think any such thing!" I saw Mum's face twist like Hannah had shot her. "It's just a formality, Hannah. He gives out leaflets like that to all his clients . . . in case . . . in case. . ." Mum looked away.

"In case he's found guilty," I said, trying to be helpful.

Only not being.

"They'll find him guilty, won't they?" Hannah yelled. "*Won't they?*"

Mum gazed at the crumbling birthday cake, and when she replied, her voice was weary, like all the fight had gone out of her. "Yes, they probably will."

But I'm going to solve the clues! I wanted to shout at them. *You don't need to worry about him being guilty.*

"They've got CCTV film of him, kids," Mum said, "waiting in some car park somewhere. It was the same night the files went missing, apparently. They taped Dad handing something over to someone, and being given an envelope of money."

I turned away. **LOOK OUT** screamed the ripped poster.

Tears slid down Hannah's cheeks. She struggled to catch her breath. "I want Dad!" she wept. "I want my dad."

Mum's face creased. "Oh, kids," she whispered. "I'm so sorry." She moved towards Hannah, and my sister let her hold her like she was a little kid again. Then Hannah backed away and tramped upstairs and I heard her plugging a number into her mobile. "Gav. It's me." More sobbing.

Mum stared again at the messed-up birthday cake, and then she snatched at the cardboard boxes where they were lined up along the wall. "It's time these were unpacked." She got a big pair of scissors and slit their brown tape, yanking up the flaps and pulling out the stuff inside, heaping them in piles; then she started to bung Auntie Hilda's things into the newly empty boxes. She pulled the war posters from the walls and rolled them into tubes

160

before dropping them in. She took down the butterflies in a frame, the metal helmet with a "W" painted on it. It was like if only she could make this house properly ours, properly home, everything would be OK.

She bundled in the horseshoes and the knitted cushions and the cracked plates from the dresser, then looked wildly at the glass case with the pigeon in it like she was about to bung that in too. She got the manky fox fur from the coat stand in the hall, the scratchy paws dangling out from the side as she forced the box lid closed. She sat on the top and slumped back, as if she had suddenly shrunk in her skin. She leaned against the wall like any second she might disappear into it.

Bones hobbled over and licked at the cake crumbs on the carpet. I gave his head a stroke. There was the sound of a car on the drive and the double headlights of Gavin's dad's four-by-four blazed at us through the window. From the music we could hear blaring, Gavin was probably at the wheel. Hannah came down the stairs. "See you later," she said, her voice all quiet, then the front door slammed and the car revved away.

Mum started to clear the table. "Can you freeze cake?" she said to the wall. Lines creased her forehead. "I'm sure you can." She sat down on the floor and stayed there. I helped her up and guided her to the fire. She stayed hunched on Dad's favourite armchair and stared at her slippers. I put a cushion behind her head and covered her with the sheepskin blanket.

She's at cracking-up point as it is.

If Mum cracked up, what would happen? My face went hot. I felt what I had to do pressing down on me. The hugeness of it. What if loving someone wasn't enough? Like with Lily and her dad. What if loving someone wasn't enough to save them?

The stuffed pigeon stared back at me with its one eye, like it knew all the answers but wasn't telling. The clock on the fireplace clicked loudly, like lots of scuttling creepy-crawlies.

The people listening in, they were probably having a good laugh at us. I felt my fists go tight. Now they'd know Hannah was losing it and Mum was at cracking-up point. They must really think they'd won.

The stupid pigeon stared and stared and stared, and suddenly I couldn't stand it any more. I swept the glass dome up from the table and marched out of the house. Down the garden I went with it pressed to my chest, and then, with a grunt, I hurled it against the nearest tree. Glass exploded outwards and sprayed over me. I felt a piece glance my face and I tasted blood.

At cracking-up point. . . Cracking-up point. . .

I stood there, panting, then stepped towards the tree and pressed my face against the freezing bark. I squeezed my eyes shut. "I want my dad," I whispered. "I want my dad."

I stared down at the crazy thing I'd done. The wind tugged at a corner of Lily's envelope, shifting it slightly along the ground. I picked it up from the mess of glass and shrivelled moss and gave it a wipe with my sleeve.

Help me

Something glinted in the snow and I picked up the scuffed bronze plaque that had been on the base. *Many miles . . . urgent flight . . . terrible weather . . . under fire . . . journey's end . . . life . . . saved.*

I looked at the bird lying in the snow, the messenger bird, and all I could see in my head was this small thing, high in the sky, dodging the bad weather and the hawks and the bullets. A speck in the sky, not knowing if he will make it or if it will do any good or if it's already too late. Only thinking of getting to the end. Only knowing that he has to make it home.

Like me, Dad, Lily. Struggling with the weight of the secrets we were carrying.

I picked the bird up. Nestled it against my jumper. How could I ever have doubted Dad, even for a second? All my anger drained out of me and shame squeezed my insides like a knot tied too tight. I was going to do whatever I could to help him. Whatever it took. They hadn't won. Not yet. Lily might not have been able to save her dad, but I wasn't giving up trying to save mine.

And the top priority now was to solve Dad's secret phone message.

I went in and laid the pigeon on the hallway cabinet,

then went up to my bedroom and hid Lily's message at the back of the secret drawer where I'd first found it. I pulled off my wet trainers and socks and got into bed. I got right under the covers, feeling warmth slowly seep through me, Dad's rushed call running through my head again.

Thirteen at last, Nathan

The petrol from BP, Nathan

I felt Bones thud down on the quilt and move around, trying to settle.

The whole book, Nathan

Important that you go there, Nathan

If I took the words, the words just before my name. . .

LAST

BP

BOOK

GO THERE

Hope you like the message in the card, Nathan. Kiss. Kiss. Kiss.

I came up from my covers gasping, rushing to get Dad's card from the front zippy pocket of my fleece.

BP BOOK

With all my LOVE for ALWAYS and ever,
Dad XXX

I scrambled out of bed and darted to my bookshelf, nearly trampling Bones in my hurry. I went along the row and pulled out the big Bletchley Park book.

It had gone quiet downstairs. The house seemed to be holding its breath.

Kiss, kiss, kiss. XXX

I turned the pages quickly, my shoulders hunched and tight, searching for the one I wanted. I got to a chapter about the mansion. Page thirty.

Page XXX.

I laid the book on the bed and crouched over it, smoothing the paper.

There was a colour photo of the ballroom we'd seen through the gap in the door, with its high, fancy ceiling and wood panel walls, and text about how the mansion was used during the war, and at the bottom of the page there was a small picture. A photo of a section of the ceiling. I almost yelped out loud. A section of the ballroom ceiling with a full moon and beams coming from it! Exactly like the design carved on the old griffins!

I could hardly believe it. Good old Dad! He'd slipped in a clue of his own, not part of Lily's trail, but something to help me with it. We had to go back to Bletchley Park! I started to leap about on the bed like it was a trampoline. Bones was not impressed.

LAST. GO THERE.

Was Dad telling me this was the last clue? Was he telling me that the evidence was hidden in the Bletchley Park ballroom – up in the painted ceiling?

I *had* to tell Sasha and Josh! I grabbed my mobile, and

then I remembered about the hacking. What I needed was a decoy.

I thumbed Sasha and Josh a text.

Evidence is @

I stopped to think.
Then I wrote

football stadium. Get 2 mine asap

I pressed *send*. Let's see how clever those hacking people were now!

My mind went back to the photo in the book. But the ballroom ceiling was being painted. Those workmen had been pretty clear. Nobody was going to be allowed in until tomorrow.

But we'd find a way in, we had to! Distract them or something. Whatever happened, we had to get in there today. Tomorrow was Dad's transfer. Tomorrow he'd be charged. I couldn't just let that happen. No, the sooner we found the evidence the better. The corrupt staff were closing in, and if it fell into their hands. . .

Worry nagged me, but I pushed it away. I'd bike round to Sasha's. I couldn't just wait about for her to get here! I took the Bletchley book downstairs and edged round Mum sleeping in the chair.

Dad might be in prison, but he was still alive. Not like

Lily's dad. Not like Lily. Percy's words weaved through my mind. *Where would we be without hope?* Was a part of Lily still here in this house somewhere, still blaming herself for not breaking the code in time, still blaming herself for not saving her dad, and willing me to save mine?

That's when I saw a shape at the window looking in through a gap in the curtains, an eye on the glass, staring right at me.

14
Friends

I yelped and jumped up, dropping the Bletchley book on my foot, while Josh looked in, his eye wide with surprise.

"Nathan?" Mum shifted in her chair. "What's going on?"

"Nothing. Sorry. I didn't mean to wake you up."

"Thank goodness you did!" Mum pulled herself up. "I'll be late for my shift!" Then she was getting her bag and her keys and she was telling me stuff as I followed her down the hall, that she'd ring soon and about the pizzas in the freezer and not to answer the door to any newspaper people because Mr Edwards had warned there might be some.

On the front step she looked at me and pulled me towards her, and I just stayed there, buried. Then her arms went loose and she walked away, and a minute later there was the sound of our car engine and I waved to her as she drove off.

"Sorry if I scared you before," Josh said, popping his

head round the door. "But *ASAP*, you said. *ASAP*." He wheeled his clattery old bike into view. "You weren't supposed to be using your mobile!"

"I'll explain everything!" I whispered. "*You* should have been here hours ago! Where were you? I gave three rings!"

Josh looked bemused. "I didn't hear any ringing."

I checked up and down the lane and pulled Josh in, making sure the front door was bolted tight. I found the big pad of paper and scribbled: You won't believe what I found out.

Really? he wrote excitedly. He took off his woolly hat and his hair stuck up at impossible angles. "Happy birthday, by the way," he said. "I was supposed to get you a card. But I forgot."

"Never mind that!" I said, getting my coat on. "Where's Sasha?"

"Here! Happy birthday, Nathan!" she called through the letter box, and I let her in and re-bolted the door. She grabbed the pad and pen.

What's this about the football stadium? What's happened? she wrote, all muffled up in her fluffy pink scarf. Why didn't you give 3 rings, Nathan?

So much for the ringing three times tactic.

Sasha took a little bottle from her pocket. "Before I forget, this is for your mum, from my mum and dad – perfume – to say they're thinking of her. I know it should be *you* getting the presents, but. . ."

I shoved the present in the pocket of my jeans. All I wanted to do was get out of the door and get to BP. "That's nice," I said as I snatched the pad back. "Tell them thanks."

We need to go! Will tell you everything on way.

We piled out of the house, huddling by the door awhile, checking there was no one about, breathing in the sharp cold. Then we set off quickly down the lane.

We stopped suddenly. There was the sound of an engine behind us, a car pulling into our drive, churning chunks of gravel under its tyres. I relaxed. It sounded like our car. *Mum back already?* I thought.

"Hang on," I told the others as I hurried back.

Mum must have got out of her shift, or maybe she'd forgotten something. That was handy, though. I could tell her where we were going and give her the bottle of perfume and. . .

But it wasn't Mum.

A shiny black and white Mini was parked by our house, sharp flakes of snow catching on its windscreen, and before I could react, a lady I'd never seen before got out. There was fur round the collar of her coat and she had a red suitcase on little clacky wheels.

"You must be Nathan," she said with a smile, and she reached out a gloved hand to try and shake mine. "I'm Mrs Atkinson." She held out an identity card.

"What do you want?" Sasha said, coming up close beside me.

The woman looked annoyed. "Didn't you get a message about me, Nathan?"

I shook my head. I felt my breathing speed up.

Mrs Atkinson gave me a pitying kind of smile. "I'm going to be looking after you while your mum's being questioned."

15
Action This Day

Sasha put a hand on my arm. "What's this about Mrs Vane being questioned?" she demanded. "How long for?"

"I've no idea, I'm afraid," the woman said. "My first objective is the care of Nathan and Hannah. I'm not part of the police side of things."

I bit my lip, fighting back the panic. They must have taken Mum in on her way to work. She'd be in a right state. Would she be charged with something too? What had Mum said about intimidation tactics? *They'll be arresting me next.*

Mrs Atkinson stamped her feet on the snowy gravel. She turned to Sasha and Josh. "Hannah will be back soon – I phoned her. I'd like some time with just the two of them, if I may?"

I saw Sasha open her mouth to argue, but Mrs Atkinson cut her off. "I'd like you to go home now, please."

You could see she meant it. She was getting rid of them, just like that! But I'd not had chance to mention anything about the phone call with Dad, or the ballroom ceiling!

But there was no way any Mrs Atkinson was going to stop me getting back to Bletchley Park. No way.

Sasha made wide eyes at me as she walked away, and Josh dragged his feet as he wheeled his bike.

"Let's go in and get warm, Nathan," said Mrs Atkinson, with a wide smile. "You can show me around the house."

I was halfway through the grand guided tour when Hannah got back.

"It's all true," she whispered when we were sat back in the sitting room and Mrs Atkinson was messing about in the kitchen. "I got a call from Mr Edwards."

"We can all stay in the rest of the day and get to know each other," said Mrs Atkinson, breezing into the room with a tray of three steaming mugs.

"I'd like to go out soon," I said. "Meet up with Sasha and Josh."

Mrs Atkinson sat herself down in Mum's chair with her cup. "We'll see," she said.

"But I need to go and. . ."

"I'd rather you both stay in," she said firmly. She took a sip of tea. "Now, Nathan. Tell me a little about yourself."

I sat on my bed, thinking hard and fuming. It had been ages before I could escape from Mrs Atkinson's "getting to know you" interrogations, and then the agonizing "light-hearted classic film" she'd insisted we watch together. I had to get to the Bletchley Park ballroom! But it was already half three. It'd be virtually closing by the time I got there now, even if it wasn't shutting early because of the snow, and even if I could leave right away. Even if Mrs Atkinson *let* me, because when I'd tried to go out, she'd stopped me in the hallway and said, *It's getting dark soon, so I'd rather you didn't*.

I'd thought about just sneaking off, but she kept checking up on me. Virtually every quarter of an hour she'd been in to ask me a question about the heating, or where the remote for the telly was, or where the dog food was kept, and other fake stuff, probably just to check I hadn't done a runner.

There were clattering noises from the kitchen. Classical music from Hannah's room. *Classical music?* I must be hearing things! I forced myself to think clearly.

That's when I remembered Percy's bunch of keys.

I'd have to go to Bletchley Park after hours; there was no way round it now. The workmen would be gone but someone might see me in the grounds, and there was no chance anyway that Mrs Atkinson would let me go out. It would have to be during the night, then, I decided. I'd have to get out of the house somehow in secret and. . .

I couldn't believe what I was planning. Breaking into Bletchley Park Mansion after dark! Me getting a criminal record – that would really help Mum's state of mind.

I got the bunch of keys out and fanned them on the duvet. Several had coloured stickers with labels like *Front Gallery, Block B Office, Hut 8 Exhibition Room*. . . There was one called *Side entrance by H11* – that must be for the gate Percy had used to leave the Bletchley Park grounds – and two others: *Mansion Main Door* and a little silver one with *Alarm* and a code pencilled on: *71940.*

My hand closed around the keys with a grim smile. This was an emergency situation, Percy, I thought. It called for emergency measures.

And all this thinking about keys had given me another idea as well.

A phone rang downstairs, a ringtone I didn't recognize, and I heard Mrs Atkinson answer it. I tiptoed from stair to stair towards the front room. She was in there, still on her mobile, her voice all low and sharp. I crept closer, not making the slightest sound. I got to the bottom step and pressed myself round the side of the door frame, straining to catch a few words. *Both upstairs . . . keeping an eye . . . making sure they don't leave the house. . .*

I felt my eyes narrow. Maybe this Mrs Atkinson wasn't everything she said she was. My back shivered. What if she was one of *Them*? What if she'd been sent to stop me finding the evidence? Come to think of it, that would fit with why she wasn't letting Hannah or me go out.

Well, two could play at that game.

Mrs Atkinson moved off into the kitchen, still on her phone, and I was in the room like a shot and my hand was in her bag feeling around for her keys, her purse. It didn't feel right, messing with her stuff like that, but what choice did I have?

I found the purse first. I undid the zip and rummaged in the compartments.

I heard a drawer open and something clatter on to the kitchen floor. Swearing. *Hurry up*, I told myself. *Come on!*

I was about to give up on the purse when, right at the back of a zipped-up part, I found a white ID card with her photo and *M. Stafford* printed on it. I waggled it to get it out . . . *HM SPECIAL SERVICES*. So I'd been right! She wasn't any stand-in mum. She was even using a false name!

Her keys were next. I lifted out the heavy clump and went through them at the speed of light until I found the key to her smart little Mini and struggled to try and get it off the key ring.

The metal ring snapped at my fingernail painfully as I rushed to twist the key off. If Mrs Atkinson found out I'd gone, at least she wouldn't be able to come after me, not straightaway anyway. *Come on!*

"I'll keep in touch," Mrs Atkinson was saying. "Yes. . . Yes. . . Right."

I heard the beep of her mobile being turned off and I leapt to the hallway and then pretended to be just coming down the stairs, banging deliberately on the last couple. I slouched in the armchair, the fake Mrs Atkinson's car key in my pocket jabbing me.

She came in to the front room and I saw she was wearing Mum's apron. "There you are!" she said, like she hadn't seen me in days.

I eyed her handbag on the chair, the slight quiver in its strap.

"I thought you might like something to eat," she said. "Now your big birthday breakfast's worn off. Call Hannah, will you?"

It hadn't worn off; it was still a solid lump in my stomach, but the table in the kitchen was all laid out. Tomato soup and a glass of milk. Toast cut into neat triangles and paper serviettes with a perfect crease. Hannah came and sat there all quiet, her hair in a long, neat plait and no make-up, in a pale blue tracksuit I hadn't seen her wear in years, sipping her watery red soup. I'd never seen her so docile.

"Hungry?"

I still didn't answer her. I didn't see why I should.

"Sit down and have your food then." Mrs Atkinson turned back to the cooker and stirred a frying pan of crouton cubes, humming along with the radio.

Hannah leaned over and caught my wrist. "Stop being *stupid*, Nathan," she hissed. "They've got Mum too now, *get it*? If we don't do what they want . . . they could say she was in on it too! Now sit down and *eat*."

I slumped on to my chair reluctantly and picked up my spoon.

Hannah eyed me suspiciously. "What are you up to,

Nathan?" she whispered. "What's all this about school projects and all that? Don't think Mum and I don't talk! What's going on?"

Been checking up on me, had she? "Nothing," I mumbled. "There's nothing going on." But Hannah was right. I shouldn't do anything to make Mrs Atkinson suspicious.

Hannah didn't look like she believed me, but she said, "Don't do anything to hack them off, that's all."

"Not hungry, Nathan?" said Mrs Atkinson. She hovered by my shoulder. "Would you like me to make you something else?"

"No, thanks, this is fine." I clamped my teeth on the toast and took a bite.

I ran the plot through in my head. I'd stay at home, keep everything normal, make Mrs Atkinson think I was just hanging around the house all depressed with nothing to do, but when she was out of the way, I'd prepare the things I needed and. . .

"I'd like to go up to my room now and telephone my boyfriend, Gavin, please," said Hannah. "Then I've some college work to do."

I tried not to choke on my toast. Hannah really was playing along. When did my big sister ever ask permission to talk to Gavin?

"That's fine," Mrs Atkinson said, while Hannah went upstairs, giving me a quick, hard stare as she left.

Mrs Atkinson opened the flap of her handbag and took

out a stick of lip balm and smeared some on her mouth. "So, Nathan, what are you doing for the rest of today? You weren't still hoping to see Sasha and Joshua again, were you?" and from the way she said it, something in her voice. . .

Sasha and Josh – it hit me – they were in real danger. It was OK me taking a risk; it was *my* dad we were trying to save after all. But if Mum could be grabbed for no good reason, or anyone they thought was involved. . .

My hand made a fist. I didn't care about myself, but I couldn't stand the thought of something happening to Sasha or Josh. I just knew I had to keep them out of it from now on. They wouldn't like it, but I'd made up my mind. I'd already got them into enough trouble.

"Nathan?" said the fake Mrs Atkinson. "I asked if you were planning to see Joshua or Sasha again today?"

"Not really," I said slowly. "But if either of them ring," I mumbled, "can you . . . would you mind telling them I'm not in? I just want to be by myself the rest of today, you know?"

"I understand," she said, looking all concerned.

"And if they call round later, can you tell them I'm asleep or something?" I asked. "They just . . . they just keep asking me stuff and I don't want to talk about it."

The woman looked at me. "If that's what you want. That's probably best. We'll stay in together! Just the three of us."

As if there was a choice. But I thought I'd better keep

her happy. "Yeah," I said. I'd stay at home with her and join in her chit-chat. I'd be a perfect boy. Later on, I'd pretend to go to bed, then slip out, get to Bletchley somehow, make it into the ballroom and then. . .

There were quite a few things that could go wrong. Like, would I really be able to switch off the burglar alarm when I went into the mansion, and might the code have changed from the one pencilled on the key, and assuming I got to the ballroom and found the ceiling design of the moon, what then? How would I get up there? Would I have enough time?

"I'm going to watch telly for a while now," Mrs Atkinson said. "There's another film I want to see."

I did well not to grimace. "I'll probably go back up to my bedroom after I've finished eating," I said. "Read awhile, if that's OK?"

"Course it is! I won't disturb you." The woman scooped up her bag and I caught my breath. She reached out and patted my arm. "Must be very stressful, all this business. Want a cup of tea to take up with you?"

All so polite and sugar sweet. She made me want to puke. But I kept playing along. I hung my head, pretending to be all grateful. "Thanks."

I finished my soup and toast quickly and went up to my room, turning my plan over and over in my mind. How was I going to get back to Bletchley after dark? I fretted. There weren't any buses from ours at that time of night. It'd take too long to walk. Calling a taxi would be too dodgy. I could bike it, though. Six miles – I could do that in, what, half an hour to an hour?

My phone rang. I looked at the screen to see who it was. Sasha. I ignored it. Josh rang a few minutes later. I ignored that too and turned my phone off. I should never have involved them in the first place. It was way too risky.

It was agony, waiting around for night, but I tried to make good use of the time. I got out my extra-warm jacket and started to put what I needed into its deep pockets: Percy's keys, my head torch, my phone, a few chocolate bars as emergency rations, and the other things I'd be wearing – my gloves, my woolly hat. I carefully ripped the moon and stars ballroom-ceiling picture out of the Bletchley Park book and put that in a pocket too. I stared at the business card Mr Edwards had given me, at the private number he'd scribbled on it. I might need to contact him, but could he be trusted? In the end I shoved the card in a pocket as well. Then I hid the jacket in my wardrobe with my boots and my bike helmet.

I tiptoed up to the attic library and dragged Auntie Hilda's old dummy across the floor. It was going to be part of my plan for tonight. It was a big job, getting it down those spiral stairs quietly, and the material of its RAF uniform kept getting snagged on the splintery banister, but I made it and bunged it in my wardrobe and as I forced the door closed on its startled face I had a fit of giggles, but that was nerves, I guess.

I lay on my bed, fretting about Mum, fretting about Dad, watching the warplane models on the ceiling circle slowly in the draught. I read some of my *Mysteries of the Universe* book to pass the time and steady my nerves, although chapters on spontaneous human combustion and messages from the dead probably weren't the best choices. I got up loads of times to double-check everything, but really I knew I was as ready as I'd ever be and eventually I decided that I should try and get some proper sleep. I pulled off my trainers and got under the duvet, setting the alarm clock on my mobile and sliding it under my pillow. Only 17:22. I closed my eyes, but I couldn't relax.

At one point I heard the doorbell go, *Match of the Day* style. Then a loud knock. Then Sasha calling me through the letter box. I lay there chewing the inside of my cheek, telling myself, *It's for their own good. It's too dangerous. Keep them out of it.* I heard Sasha's voice raised in surprise. Mrs Atkinson's voice, all angry. The door banging shut.

I breathed out. More ringing, knocking, shouting. I turned over and covered my ears with my hands, trying to block the sounds out. *Go away!*

Eventually it went quiet. I lay there, still trying to sleep. I think I must have dropped off a few times, but I kept waking up, worried about what time it was, worried that it was Monday morning already and I was too late. But the clock crawled on . . . 18:07 . . . 18:08 . . . 18:09. . . Somehow it got to 19:34 and I heard Hannah calling me and I went down and forced myself to eat even more food

Mrs Atkinson had made, like she was trying to fatten us up or something: a supper of corned beef from a tin and lumpy mashed potatoes, then rice pudding with a splat of red jam. But I reckoned I needed all the energy I could get for tonight.

Hannah didn't say much, but she was all pale and kept giving me looks across the table, and slipped up to the bathroom while Mrs Atkinson was dolloping out the rice pudding and was away ages.

"I'll make us cocoa," Hannah offered after we'd cleared the plates, the creep, and Mrs Atkinson beamed at her.

I went back to bed, listening to the sound of the telly through the floorboards. Later I heard Mrs Atkinson tramping upstairs and my door opening a chink as she looked in at me pretending to be asleep. The door closed quietly. There was the sound of a tap running in the bathroom, the door to Mum and Dad's bedroom swinging open.

I lay there, eyes snapped wide. *Just a little longer*, I told myself. *Be ready*.

I pulled the curtain open and let the full moon's light flood in. I looked out at the garden, at the outline of the well, the shed, the air-raid shelter. The big moon behind the tree branches made the garden sparkle.

The pane in front of me shook, making me spring back from the window, and Bones dropped down with a yowl. The glass rattled again, like something had been thrown against it. I tried to look out, but it was hard to see. Mrs

Atkinson must have heard that; surely she would be in any second! I waited. Nothing. I lifted the latch and yanked the window open.

Two figures stood in the dark garden staring up at me, their eyes lit like ghosts: Sasha and Josh, who was about to lob another handful of gravel.

"Why wouldn't you answer your phone?" Sasha hissed.

I said nothing.

"*Why*, Nathan?"

I stuck my head out as far as I could and pulled my window closed a bit.

"It's not safe," I muttered. "They might hear."

"We don't *care* about them hearing!" she said. "We already knew it wasn't safe, so why push us out?" she demanded.

I said nothing.

"Tell us!"

"The trail's off," I mumbled. "Dad told me it was all a fake."

"Rubbish!" Sasha snapped back. "I don't believe you. Did someone threaten you?"

I won't let anything happen to you, I promised them in my head.

"Because if they did," Sasha stuttered, "even if they're on to us, you're not pushing us out, Nathan!" Her voice was angry. I saw her swot a tear from her cheek. "Not after everything we've been through. Whatever they said to

184

you, I don't care. *I don't care!* We're in this *together*!"

"It's true, Nathan."

I looked at Josh, his face pinched up with fear, shivering in his too-thin coat. And Sasha, her shoulders hunched in the cold. I saw my friends, my best friends, looking up at me, knowing what they were risking, and in that moment it was like something exploded in my chest. Like I was buried under rubble and the weight of it was pressing down on me, and everyone else had gone, but the two of them were still trying to find me, not giving up on me.

I swallowed, then tried to think straight. I thought about the bugs listening in. "I'm leaving for the stadium at midnight," I said loudly. "Be here with your bikes, and no noise."

Sasha set her mouth into a hard line. "I'm in," she said, and I saw Josh nod once.

With a single nod back, I watched them slip away, melting into the moonlight as I pulled the window shut.

16
Miles to Go Before I Sleep

My alarm vibrated through my pillow and I sat up with a gasp. I felt freezing. My duvet had come off and the sheet was damp with sweat. I fumbled under the pillow. 23:50, my clock said. Ten to midnight. It was time.

The moon was high and bright, filling my room with silver. I got out of bed and got dressed. Then I lugged the mannequin from my wardrobe and dragged it under the covers. I'd have to hope that was enough to fool Mrs Atkinson if she looked in on me.

No sound from the house. I pulled on my padded jacket, my boots, my hat, my gloves. I got my bike helmet out and headed downstairs. Mum and Dad's bedroom door was slightly open and there was snoring coming from inside. Not keeping watch very well, was she, I thought with satisfaction.

I tiptoed down to the front room and stopped. Was

that the noise of a door opening, footsteps on the stairs? I stayed there, my ears straining. Nothing.

I slipped out of the house and locked the door behind me. I froze. Had that curtain moved upstairs? I waited, hardly breathing, half expecting the woman to come storming after me any second, but the house stayed silent. I turned to go, although it didn't feel right, leaving Hannah there by herself.

"Nathan?"

Josh's worried face appeared from the shadows with his bike. He was wearing his helmet strapped tight under his chin, like he was in a war zone. "Where's Sasha?" I whispered.

Josh peered up the moonlit lane. "Maybe she got delayed."

We gave her some extra time. At one point a car drove slowly past our house, sending headlights on to the bare treetops, and we had to crouch low in the bushes until it was out of sight. Somewhere close, an owl hooted. We tried to ring Sasha, but her phone was off. I looked at my watch. "We can't wait any more. We have to get going!"

We set off, bracing ourselves against the cold. I'd decided to bike along the bridleway, the wide footpath that went across fields and through patches of woodland all the way to the edge of town. I wanted to get off the road as soon as possible. Ten minutes it might take to get to the start of the bridleway; then maybe another forty minutes to Bletchley, an hour tops.

It was easy to see the way in the moonlight, but the edge of the road was slippery with snow and so we cycled up on the verge, the icy blades of grass crackling under our tyres. I couldn't stop thinking about Sasha. What if something had happened to her on the way?

I was about to turn back when I heard a bike behind us and Sasha appeared all out of breath and I smiled wide with relief. "Sorry," she panted. "It was hard to get away. I followed your tyre tracks."

"What about your mum and dad?" I said, as we picked up speed, shouting over the noise of the bikes and the rushing air.

"I pretended to go to bed, then locked my bedroom door and took the out-the-window-and-on-to-the-garage-roof route," she said. "Which way are we going to the stadium?"

"We're not going to the stadium."

"But you said. . . Oh, I get it!" Sasha flashed me a grin. "You wanted them to think that! Where, then?"

"Bletchley Park."

I flashed Percy's bunch of keys, and Josh swerved so much he nearly came off his bike.

I explained all about my phone call with Dad and told them about the photo in the Bletchley Park book, and how the ceiling design in the ballroom matched the design carved on the griffins; how Dad had seemed to be telling me it was the last clue; the end of the trail. They listened as we sped on, Josh nodding his head like it was on a spring. When I glanced at their faces in the moonlight, I saw they were shocked and scared, but they never slowed down once.

"We need to get to the bridleway," I said. "If anyone drives past on this stretch of road, they're bound to see us, so we need to get a move on!"

We went quickly down the snowy lane. Past the village war memorial with poppy wreaths on its steps. Fast along packed-down snow towards the place where we could join the off-road track.

"I can hear a car coming!" Josh shouted through his scarf, his legs going crazy on his rubbish bike. He was right. It was in the distance still, but definitely heading our way. We had to get off the road!

We put on a spurt of speed, heading for the gap in the hedge and the gateposts where the track started. How far was it? Another hundred metres? It was hard to tell in the dark. I clicked on my head torch and zoomed forward, pushing the pedals down hard.

The car was much closer; I could see its headlamps now as it wound its way down the hill towards us. We found the posts and veered through, me nearly coming off as I made the turn. The headlights caught at nearby branches and I signalled wildly for Sasha and Josh to get under the trees.

"Kill your light!" she hissed.

Just in time. A car swept past, its headlights blazing, almost blinding us. We hid in the thicket, watching it go.

"Did you get a look at the car?" I said. Had it got tinted windows? I fretted. It couldn't have been Mrs Atkinson – I still had the key of her Mini. Had she realized I'd gone already? Could she have called someone? Maybe she'd been faking being asleep.

"Hang on." I pulled my mobile from my jacket pocket and brought up the message box. I started to type.

"Don't!" yelped Josh, trying to grab my arm. "Remember you shouldn't be using that!"

I shrugged him off, continuing with the message. "I know. It's OK. It's another decoy."

Am by west gate of stadium. Where r u?

There. I sent the message to Sasha, and a few seconds later I heard her phone beep as she received it. "Come on!" I shouted. We headed off up the bridleway.

We biked along the untouched snow. It was slower going than the road, but it felt good to be on my bike. I felt the power of it under me as I forced the pedals round. The bridleway was wide and snowy smooth. The moonlight carved huge shadows on every bump, but it was enough to see by. We didn't need lights. Tree branches seemed to point the way. My plan was working! A giddy feeling swept through me, and I let the noise of my flapping jacket drown out any niggling doubts.

I saw a gleam in Sasha's eyes as we raced each other between the trees. We were going fast. Frosty branches quivered in the wind as we sped past. We went up across a big field, then back down to a straight stretch between the trees.

Not far now. I put on a spurt of speed. Was Sasha or Josh shouting something behind me? It was hard to hear over the sound of the rushing wind.

I saw it too late.

The bend in the track, sharp to the right. Too sharp. I yanked the brakes and started to slow, but I felt the wheels spin in the ice and the bike gave a grinding sound and I twisted to keep control, but I was turning too much and the bike went from under me. I came off and slammed down, sliding and turning along the snow, a terrible pain shooting down my right arm.

I lay there staring up at the stars. Then I heard Joshua gabbling in my ear and my elbow was really hurting and I saw my bike on the ground and my head torch near it, its beam shooting into the sky.

My helmet had a dint in it, but better that than my head, as Josh pointed out as he dragged me up. My arm hurt loads as I bent it, but at least I *could* bend it.

I took it more carefully from then on and we lost tonnes of time. My arm was in agony, but I couldn't stop now. We reached the outskirts of town and weaved our way down the quiet backstreets, getting closer to Bletchley Park. The wind picked up. We hid the bikes and helmets in a dark alley behind some big bins and carried on by foot, our feet slipping on the frozen pavement as we tried to keep to the shadows.

I focused on what I had to do: unlock the fence gate, get into the mansion and disable the alarms. I didn't even want to think about what would happen if they went off. "Find the ceiling design of the moon," I muttered to myself.

"We should keep our gloves on at all times," said Josh as we hurried along on the snow, his luminous trainers catching the moonlight. "Avoid leaving any fingerprints."

I swallowed. Breaking and entering. No going back.

We arrived at Bletchley Park with its chain-link fence and a security light blazing. We went along to the side entrance we'd seen Percy use, my bad arm throbbing as I flexed my fingers.

Josh shone the torch for me and I stuck the side entrance key in the lock and tried to turn it. But it was too stiff. We exchanged looks.

"Try again!" said Sasha.

I found myself sweating. What if it didn't work? What if the key was for a different gate? I wished I'd worn my thinner gloves. The padded fingers were too fat to handle the key properly. I waggled them off. "Forget fingerprints," I said. What if this outside gate was alarmed as well? I thought suddenly. I didn't think I had a key for that.

I looked behind us. I was sure I'd heard something; that a shadow had moved back there.

A scary idea came to me. I got my mobile from my pocket and brought up Lily's last message.

07700900583

This is Lily. Help me Nath. . .

"What are you *doing*?" hissed Sasha. "There's no time for more decoys!"

I didn't answer her. I clicked CALL.

There was a second or two while the phone connected, then a second or two for what I was hearing to sink in.

A ringing sounded through the air. Close by and getting closer, fast. I fumbled to get the key in the lock. The ringing got nearer, and we all heard it now: muffled thuds as the ringing got louder and louder. Big boots clumping on snow, heading straight towards us.

Josh covered his ears. "Hurry!"

I forced the key with a cry. There was a click and the lock jolted open. I pushed the gate and we tumbled through, slamming it locked behind us. I ran fast away from the fence under the glaring security light, desperate to find somewhere to hide, slipping on puddles, cracking the ice, and not ever looking back once.

17
A Gilded Ceiling

We crouched between the side of a hut and a brick wall. Our panting echoed eerily along the narrow space we were wedged into.

The wall was freezing against my back. How had *They* found out where we were? I'd thought I'd been so clever. Dad's words pecked at me as my heart pounded in my chest. *It's dangerous . . . dangerous. . .*

I shuffled forward and peered round the side of the hut. I couldn't make anything out. But everything looked so different at night; so different in the moonlight. I managed to get my bearings and edged out. "This way," I said.

I tried the Lily number a couple more times as we scuttled along, in case we heard the ring again – but whoever had it must have turned the phone off. It was a horrible thought, though – Them waiting outside, waiting patiently for us to find Dad's evidence. Or Them finding a way in and. . . I tried not to think about it.

We went past some kind of memorial stone, making too much noise on the icy pebbles. I thought about the security guard in his little booth by the gate. Would he be on duty all night? He might do his rounds soon. We crossed a tarmac courtyard and the mansion loomed up in front of us, and it was only when I reached the door and turned to check on Sasha and Josh that I realized how thick I'd been.

Footprints! I groaned. Three sets of footprints, one with an excellent tread. We'd left a nice, clear trail all the way from the gate right to here! But what could we do about it now? We had to go on.

I had the keys ready. The one for the front door and the one for the alarm. The metal felt icy against my bare skin. I ran the alarm code through my head to make sure I had it exactly right. There wouldn't be any second chances. *7-1-9-4-0.*

"What if the alarm code's been changed?" hissed Josh.

Yes, what if the code *had* been changed since the forgetful Percy pencilled it in on his key? There was a lump in my throat that wouldn't go away. "Ready?" I said, and Sasha nodded.

"Get your gloves back on, though, please, Nathan," said Josh. "If you leave your prints anywhere, that's one hundred per cent evidence in a court of law!"

I unlocked the front door and straightaway I heard the *bip-bip-bip* of the alarm warning. "Where's the box?"

"There!"

I sprang over to a code pad on the wall, the alarm key ready. I slipped it in and then I typed the numbers: *7* . . . *1*. . . So far so good, but I really wished I'd worn my thinner gloves. The fingers were too chunky to press the keys properly and each press was painfully slow. I felt like I was trying to defuse a bomb.

The *bip-bip-bip*, got faster, louder. I started to waggle a glove off. "Don't touch it with your actual finger!" cried Josh.

I kept the glove on. *9*. . . The *bip-bip-bip* was hideously fast and shrill now.

"Hurry!" Josh covered his ears.

4. . . One continuous sound. . . I gritted my teeth and. . . *0*.

Silence.

I patted Josh on the shoulder and pointed to the door at the end of the hallway. "It's that way," I wheezed, and we crept through the rooms, everywhere bathed in the same pale moonlight.

"What was that?" The three of us stood very still. The sound of a door thudding shut? We hurried on.

"Through here," I said. The smell of drying paint got stronger. We found the ballroom entrance, the yellow and black tape still across it and wobbling in a draught. *DANGER DANGER DANGER*.

We pushed the door open and our torch beams made weird, long shadows on the dark wooden panels of the walls.

The tall stepladder still stood in the middle of the room, leading up the side of the scaffolding to a wooden ledge close to the ceiling. Dark velvet curtains hung mummified in plastic, and there were tins of paint and plastic bottles and glass jars, and paintbrushes and rollers soaking in buckets smelling of turps. There was a big metal toolbox, with spanners and chisels and screwdrivers spilling from it.

I looked at the high ceiling with its clusters of posh lights, with designs of curving white leaves and flowers and shells on shining gold backgrounds. Ghostly faces with gaping mouths stared down. I got out the page from the Bletchley book and smoothed it out, and we walked about, shining our torches, searching for a match.

Where *was* it? The floor's paint-splattered sheets wrinkled as we stepped over them. There were so many designs, all so high up. I swallowed and forced myself to keep looking.

"Here!" Sasha stood in front of dark wooden pillars rising up into a double archway. I rushed over and stared at where she was pointing. I had to take a few steps back and then let out a gasp. I saw it too! The design we were looking for. The full moon with a crescent inside it and beams coming out.

Sasha climbed some rungs of the ladder. "Can you see anything else?"

I stared, getting a crick in my neck. It was hard to get a proper view from the ground.

"We have to get up there and examine it more closely," said Josh.

I stayed rooted to the floor. Had Dad really wanted me to go up there, knowing how much I hated heights?

"If we climb the stepladder we can get to the start of that painting ledge and walk along straight to the bit of ceiling we need, OK?" Sasha made it all sound so easy, but my insides churned.

"Nathan doesn't do high up stuff, Sasha, remember?" Josh said to her out of the corner of his mouth, like that would mean I wouldn't hear him. "He might get paralysed with fear halfway and get stuck."

Stop being so stupid, I told myself. It wasn't that high, really, was it? My teeth chattered. My arm throbbed. "*I* should do it," I said. "It's up to me to go."

"You *sure*?" Sasha and Josh drew back to let me pass. I paused, then thumped a foot on to the bottom rung of the ladder. *It's not that high*, I told myself. *Only to the ceiling. A few metres.* But the higher I got up the metal steps, the more it was like my feet were turning into chunks of metal themselves. My head swam and I felt like throwing up. Then I felt hands on my feet, and my friends were helping me back down.

"Don't worry," said Sasha. "You hurt your arm anyway. You need two good arms for this job. We'll go."

I felt such a failure.

Sasha went over to the ladder and shook the bottom to check it was stable, then held the metal handrails.

She climbed quickly to the top and paused a moment, checking her balance; then my skin shuddered as she swung herself on to the wooden ledge. "Your turn, Josh."

He climbed on to the scaffolding, his thin body moving easily from one strut to the next. I watched them walk along the wooden platform towards the moon design, me wincing every time they took a step. Closer they went, to within reaching distance. . .

The first sign that something was wrong was the noise.

There was a strange creaking, and then the scraping, grating sound of metal against metal. Sasha stopped dead. The steel bars trembled and growled. Josh shouted in fear as the scaffolding shifted.

I saw it now: a latch that was supposed to clasp one rod of the scaffold to another. It was unhooked, dangling down on its length of rope. Maybe the workmen left it like that, ready for quick dismantling in the morning.

Josh clung to a strut. "A five-and-a-half-metre fall, I'd estimate," he was gibbering to himself. "Maybe six." Sasha's mouth was fixed in a silent scream.

The scaffolding could go any second. "Don't move!" I shouted, panic choking my voice.

A terrible image leapt into my mind – Sasha and Josh sprawled on the ballroom floor. I remembered my promise to them from my bedroom window: *I won't let anything happen to you*. It was my fault they were here. My fault. I had to help them; I had to climb the ladder and go along the ledge. It was the only way. A voice spoke inside me, stern and clear, telling me exactly what to do. *Latch the hook back in place. Take two steps.* That was all. *Two small steps.*

I climbed the ladder, one foot after the other. Somehow I got to the top rung. I tilted my chin up and reached for the wooden ledge with a foot. The growling steel started to shriek. I felt a horrible wobble in the wood as my foot made contact.

I pressed my back against the wall as I shuffled along the ledge towards the latch, feeling with my fingertips as I tried to get a grip on the smooth panels. Waves of pain shot up my bad arm as I made clumsy sideways steps. I kept my eyes fixed on the opposite side of the ceiling, desperate not to look down.

I came to a stop, gasping for air. I couldn't go on. I just couldn't.

The scaffolding moved to one side, then the other. I heard Sasha scream for real, the sound echoing round the walls.

I did another shuffle. Then another. The dangling latch was almost within reach. I'd have to use my right hand, though. My arm felt like it was on fire as I stretched it out. My fingers closed around the latch. With a grunt I heaved it up and wrenched it back into the metal loop. . .

The scaffolding shuddered to a stop.

I leaned my head against the wall, panting. The room swayed and I balanced there, willing it to go still.

"Thanks, Nathan," Josh said quietly.

"You go down," I croaked across to them. "I'll look around the design."

Sasha frowned. "No, we'll help you—"

"*Please*," I interrupted, my face tight. "Just get down. Please."

They must have heard the edge in my voice and got the message. I watched them make their way carefully down the scaffolding to the ground; then I adjusted my head torch and fixed my eyes on the moon with its stretching beams.

There was nothing obvious. I couldn't see any stars in the ceiling design, or anywhere near. The touching-up paint was still sticky and I got gold on my fingertips as I felt around. I ran my hand along the wooden edges of the painted piece, but there was nothing. What was I expecting – a secret drawer pinging out; the ceiling sliding back to reveal a hidden compartment, like you see in films, and a nice fat file of papers with **EVIDENCE** stamped on it?

I glanced down at Sasha and Josh. Bad idea. I took a few seconds to steady myself.

Josh gave me a nod of encouragement and I searched the design some more. "How can there be anything hidden in that?" I muttered. I scraped at the plaster with my fingertips. *They've all led you on a nutty wild goose chase after all, haven't they, Nathan? A trail going nowhere. What are you going to do now, eh?*

I stood there on the top rung of the ladder, biting my lip. There had to be something up here. I'd find it. If I could just stop being too worried and too thick. . .

Sasha looked up at me and her face was kind, but her head was shaking from side to side, and for the first time I saw doubt like a mask over her face. "Maybe it's a dead end," she said gently. "Or maybe someone got here before us. Maybe the painters found it when they were up there."

I let my arms slump to my sides. I dropped my head down to my chest. For a tiny moment the beam of my head torch lined up with the central beam from the moon on the ceiling. . .

And that was when I saw it.

18
Star Gazing

Along the moonbeam, the torchlight went, down the wood-covered wall, through the arch. "Look at that wooden panel!" I whispered in a frenzy, keeping my torch right on it like a searchlight. My arm ached like mad, but I didn't care. "Look there!"

"What?" Sasha gave me a funny look, then gasped and ran over to a panel at floor level. Josh knelt by Sasha. They're stars, Nathan," he said. "Stars!"

I got off the platform and eased myself down the ladder. My legs still wobbly, I stumbled over to join the others.

You wouldn't see the stars unless they were pointed out. Even then, only if the light was at a certain angle and you looked at them a certain way. I ran my fingers over the large, smooth rectangle. In each of its four corners was a star, four wooden inlays of a slightly lighter colour to the rest, the only thing to mark the panel out from the hundreds of others.

Josh pressed his ear against the wood and tapped along it with his knuckles. "It seems to be hollow inside!" He knocked on more wall. "I think the space goes back quite a long way."

I scraped at the panel with my fingertips. There was a tiny gap at the bottom of it and when I got my nails in there and pulled, it shifted just ever so slightly. Blood raced in my ears. "We need to open it," I said, and we fiddled around to get a grip in the thin slit.

I heard the sound of footsteps on the gravel outside. "Turn off the torches!" I said. "Now!" I ran across the ballroom floor, stumbling on the splatter sheets. I remembered the tools left by the workmen and went to grab a chisel. I sprinted back and dug the end in the crack to try and lever the panel up.

There was no time to be scared; no time to bother about how sore my arm was. We knelt shoulder to shoulder, our fingertips wedged in the bottom crack, and together we pulled upwards.

There was the definite sound of a door creaking open in a nearby room. Creeping footsteps.

We pulled again and the panel jolted up, sliding semi-smoothly over the panel above it, leaving just enough room to get through. Without thinking, I shoved Josh in. Sasha went next. I followed.

There was someone just outside the ballroom door. I saw their shadowy shape appear as I slid the panel quietly shut, trapping us behind it in total, utter darkness.

19

The Secret Room

We crouched together in the dark, cold space, listening. I strained my ears for any sound, but there was none, just the three of us, struggling to control our breathing. Not even a chink of moonlight showed along the panel we'd come through. There was a dense smell of wood and stale air and it felt like being in a coffin. We waited and we listened, not daring to move. I heard Josh sneeze; Sasha coughed. I pressed my knees against my stomach, my arm tight with cramp.

"Do you think they've gone?" I whispered at last, my voice sounding all muffled.

"Think so," said Sasha. "Hope so."

"If the light can't get in," mumbled Josh. "Then our light won't get out." I heard him nibbling at his nails. "This place must be totally sealed."

I reached for my forehead and turned on my torch with

a click. "Where *are* we?" Grey specks swirled in the beam. The others put their torches on and we sat there in the middle of the floor, looking around in disbelief.

We were in a tiny room with a bare wooden floor. It was more like a big box than a room, like a prison cell without any windows, with a reddish leathery covering on the walls, but with just about enough space to stand up in. Slowly, I got to my feet, shaking the pins and needles from my legs.

"I think this place might be soundproof as well," whispered Josh. He pressed the walls of the room and when I felt them, they were kind of spongy under my fingers, padded with something or other and nailed in place. "But best not to be too loud, just in case," he said.

I kept gazing around. Amazement pushed out my fear. We'd worked it out! This was where Lily's trail had brought us, the end of the trail Dad had wanted me to follow. The evidence had to be in here, right?

"A secret room slap bang in the middle of Bletchley Park," said Josh, wiping a cobweb off his head where he'd brushed against the low ceiling. "It's unbelievable!" He hopped about. "Imagine when I tell Percy. He's bound to let us off stealing his keys, and maybe even breaking and entering!"

We started to search, our torch beams criss-crossing over the squishy walls. My light came to rest on something in a corner. I went closer and knelt over it. It was a honey-coloured wooden box, about the size of a small suitcase, with a little metal latch on the lid to seal it closed. I tried to lift the whole thing, but it was heavier than I expected and there was no way I could with my bad arm. My throat pulsed as I pulled back the latch and opened the lid.

"You're not going to believe this," I said.

Sasha and Josh were crouched next to me in an instant. A silence fell over the three of us, as if the thing in the box were giving out some secret, hypnotic signal.

"You've got to be kidding me!" said Sasha.

"Lily never stole it," I whispered. "It was here all along."

Josh just stared, his eyes wide and round.

It was an Enigma Machine. An Enigma Machine like the one in the glass case in the exhibition centre, with the two keyboards and the three dials, and a window by each of the dials set to A—A—A.

But how could an Enigma Machine be Dad's evidence?

"Help me check the box," I urged, and we bent over it, scanning its parts.

Sasha lifted up a twisty wire attached to the back with an old-fashioned-looking plug on the end.

"I don't think this was Lily's." Josh lifted out a sheet of paper. There were words biroed across the top:

Leon Vane was here - September 1971

I grabbed the paper off him. "Dad was here . . . when he was thirteen!" My chest thudded as I scanned the page. It had a diagram of the Enigma Machine, with labels pointing to different bits of it. More writing said *the settings when I found it*, but there was no sign of any evidence. Where *was* it? I was about to shove Dad's paper to one side when I noticed something on the diagram.

"There's a front part, remember!" I cried, forgetting to be quiet. "Open it! Open it!"

We felt the wood at the front of the Enigma Machine and tugged and a piece creaked down to reveal a panel with all these holes marked with capital letters, and a couple of wires pegged in.

And there was something wedged beside the pegs.

I rushed to get it, but Sasha snatched it from the box before me and waved it in the air, smirking.

A phone. It was a phone.

I caught my breath.

I'd know it anywhere.

Dad's

mobile

phone.

I couldn't take my eyes off it. I heard Mr Edwards in his office. *If we find the evidence, it could prove Leon's innocence.*

Dad's phone!

Sasha gave it to me and I cradled it against my coat. I sat there a moment with my eyes closed, my back flat against the squashy wall, clutching it in my two hands.

"It's the snazzy new thing he showed us that time, right?" cried Sasha. "A touch screen with all the apps."

"Turn it on! Turn it on!" urged Josh, and I scrambled to find the power button.

The screen glowed into life. Icons peppered the screen. I tapped *Stored Files* and held my breath. A list flashed up – I scrolled down, blinking – a very long list. There were documents and audio files and images and video footage, and the stored stuff had names like *suspect3_meets_buyer* and *suspect1_phone_call* and *shredded_memo* and *evidence_13d*!

I laughed out loud. This was it. This was definitely it! Everything we needed to get Dad off – not a shadow of a doubt!

I felt dizzy with relief. We'd done it. We'd really done it.

"Nathan." Sasha's arm was round me. Josh was sitting close.

"Thanks, guys," I managed. "Thanks."

We sat like that a while, and then Sasha spoke. "So, then. What do we do now?"

I looked at her. I'd been so busy thinking about *finding* the evidence, I hadn't really thought what we were supposed to do with the evidence when we found it.

I thought of Mr Edwards's business card in my pocket; the private number to ring him on. Whose side was he really one? Mr Edwards and Dad had been at school together, I couldn't help thinking; that meant something, didn't it? He'd warned me about his office and my house being bugged.

"We could phone Dad's solicitor," I said uncertainly.

"But we think he was got at, remember?" cried Josh. "They threatened his kids!"

"We don't know that for sure," I said. "Besides, I really don't know who else we can go to. We can't wait around in here for ever, but if we leave this room. . ."

The three of us stared at the panel we'd rushed in through, and Josh went an ashy colour. Who knew what was waiting for us out *there*.

I pummelled a bit of wall in frustration, then chewed my knuckles. Dad *should* have told me what to do with the phone when I found it! Surely he must have thought that through. I dredged back through my last conversation with him. Was there anything else he'd said? Could there have been more to his message? I remembered his edgy question: *Have I been in the papers?* Then: *The press have the story already. . .*

I sprang up. Dad *had* told me what to do with the evidence! *Soon they'll all have the whole story, Nathan.* He wanted me to take it to the papers!

"Of course!" said Josh when I told them. "The papers will blow this thing wide open! We should have thought of that. I know – we can email the evidence to them from here – send all the files electronically!" He took Dad's phone from me. "All we have to do is use this to get on the Internet and find the emails for the editors of all the main newspapers and then. . ."

He stopped; tapped at the screen; rotated the whole

thing one way, then the other. "It's gone off, Nathan," he said, his voice all small. "The battery's totally flat."

"That's decided, then," said Sasha dryly.

I took a breath. "Mr Edwards," I said. It had to be.

"We know I can't use my phone, though." I pulled out the business card he'd slipped me, and we huddled together in the greenish light of Sasha's mobile while I dialled the number.

It rang a while, then Mr Edwards came on the line, his voice all strained and tired. "Nathan?" He was suddenly alert as he realised it was me. I put him on speaker so Sasha and Josh could hear as well. I quickly filled him in. He gasped, then paused, then spoke without stopping.

"The ballroom, you say? It seems beyond belief! A panel lifts up? We can't talk long. They could be tracing the call my end. This is very tricky. I have to tread very carefully, you understand. I can't be seen to be involved in any unorthodox practice – I wouldn't want to compromise your father's case. Listen, hold on until morning. There's people in the force I trust. I'll send people to get you out first thing in the morning as soon as Bletchley Park opens – you're there illegally, remember. If we mess up now, the evidence on the phone could be inadmissible and you can say goodbye to your dad going free. Stay where you are. Don't move from there! I'll get help to you first thing in the morning." The line went dead.

"You heard what he said." I put Sasha's phone in my coat pocket and pulled out the chocolate bars I'd brought and shared them out. "We have to wait, so here's some emergency rations."

"I'm not very good with patience," said Josh, unwrapping his and taking a huge bite. I saw one of his hands was shaking.

It was a lot colder in the secret room now, and we huddled together for warmth as we munched. I noticed how much dimmer my head torch was. I thought about Dad's dead phone. "Best save the batteries," I said. I imagined sitting for hours in the pitch black and it wasn't a nice thought. "Only keep one on at a time."

All we heard was our breathing. No sounds came from outside the secret room, nothing, but somehow it was worse, that silence. Josh's leg twitched. All this waiting, waiting. I turned Dad's phone in my hand, thinking about all that vital evidence stored up in such a small thing. The only thing that could save him.

I looked at my watch. Twenty past two.

"Mr Edwards will come and help us, won't he, Nathan?" whispered Josh, his face scrunched up with anxiety.

I nodded sheepishly. *Yes. Mr Edwards will come with help*, I told myself. *He will*.

Old doubts sprang up about the solicitor – why hadn't Dad just told *him* where the evidence was? Everything would have been so much easier if he had. *Mr Edwards will come with help*, I told myself again, *stop worrying*, but I suddenly couldn't help thinking I'd just made a mistake. A very bad mistake.

213

"When will he be here?" said Josh. "I'll need to get out of here soon! If those corrupt staff find us here. . ." His eyes rolled in terror. All those hours of television, finally having their effect.

"It's OK, Josh," I said. "We have to sit tight." Now definitely wasn't the time to get claustrophobic.

Josh sat there mumbling to himself. Sasha stroked his arm, raising her eyebrows at me. I had to get his mind on something else; get him sidetracked, stop him freaking out. Stop all of us freaking out.

I jabbed a thumb at the Enigma Machine in its box. "So Lily never stole it after all, eh, Josh?"

"Yeah, Josh," said Sasha, catching on. "It was in here all along, hey? Right under their noses!"

Josh gave a weak smile and nodded.

We shuffled him over to it and Sasha ran her fingers over the keys. "Lily just hid it here, do you reckon, so she could carry on working on the codes? They wouldn't let her do extra shifts, remember? But how did she even know this place existed, do you think?"

"A lot of old mansion houses have a secret room," said Josh quietly. "Maybe Lily came across it by accident; I saw a film with that in once." He gazed around. "But I've no idea how she smuggled the Enigma Machine in here, or how she got in and out from the panel without anyone seeing."

"But you can't really blame her for taking it, can you?" said Sasha. "I mean, her dad was the only family she had left. She was desperate to crack the codes in time, and if they stopped her from working longer hours. . ."

"Why didn't she admit it was here, though, when she was arrested?" Josh said. He was getting all agitated again. "That's the part I still don't understand. They wouldn't have called her a traitor if they knew what she was *really* using the Enigma Machine for." His voice went a pitch higher. "So why not tell them?"

"I don't know, Josh." Sasha nibbled the last of her chocolate bar, eyeing him. "But do you think Nathan's dad knows anything about the Coventry side of the story?" she added quickly. She pulled her hat lower and blew on her gloves. "Think about it – maybe as far as he's concerned, finding the Enigma Machine in here proved Lily was guilty."

I nodded. Maybe Dad had assumed Lily was a traitor.

"I'm cold," complained Josh suddenly, and he started walking about, blowing on his hands, wrapped up tight in his scarf. In a few strides he was across the room and his face was almost pressed against the padded wall. Then he swivelled round and paced back. Up he went, down he went. Up, down, up, down, pacing the room as much as you can when it's the size of a large crate.

"Nathan." Sasha shot an alarmed look at me. "If we don't calm him down soon, he could go into a right panic."

Josh had stopped pacing. He stood peering at the padded wall, at where a sliver of fabric had come loose. A nail was missing, and we watched as Josh peeled a strip of the padding back. Grey foamy stuff poured out from inside.

"Nathan ,"said Sasha. "He's *losing it!*"

"I think I've found something else," said Josh, and when I went to look at the bare wood underneath. . .

I

There was something scratched on! A letter?

Sasha and I helped him bend the padding back more and there was the groan of leather and a nail pinged out on to the floor.

"Josh, you're a genius," I told him, and he went red with pride.

Ini. . .

"No way!" breathed Sasha as we tugged the padding off.

Initially you. . .

We stared at each other.

Initially you must set the three.

But it didn't end there. There were more letters. We yanked the tightly nailed fabric, pulling out handfuls of grey foam like there was no tomorrow. We should have thought about things better, that we were taking off the soundproofing, that with that gone anyone in the ballroom would hear us through the wall. But we were too excited. We didn't think. Not until it was too late.

QANHV XGHPF WYYIN. . . Round the walls the Enigma code went. Fistfuls of foam and pinging nails flew across the secret room. On and on in a long, straight line. XXOIY RBODF BSRQC ALRPA XCNJE. We tore away the padding, revealing more and more letters. LOWDC RZZGT PLFVJ UQAZC IJGHD CAW. . .

Round and round the letters went, all written in Lily's same style – I recognized it from her notebook, her message, the engraving on the milestone; Lily had definitely written them – until at last we'd gone full circle and we were back to where we started.

Initially you must set the three.

And there was a date scratched underneath.

December 1940.

Sasha ran her fingers round the row of letters. "Is it the Enigma code Lily was trying to crack, do you think?" she whispered. "A dead duck she never managed to work out?"

I knew one thing – it was a message Lily scratched here

before she was arrested, just before she died; the date proved that. Somehow she must have got underneath the soundproofing; replaced the foam over it afterwards. What might the message say? Might it explain why she set the trail in the first place; why she never told the Bletchley people about this secret room?

What if we could know the truth? Clear her name or something.

"Hey, Josh, wouldn't it be great if we could work this out?" I said.

At the very least it would help focus him on something else that wasn't pacing and fretting and being scared to death. We still had a good few hours to kill, after all. Besides, I wanted to know the truth. Lily had got to me. *Help me*, her first words had been, speaking to me from the past.

"Yes, Josh," Sasha said. "What do you say?"

"We absolutely *have* to decode it," Josh said, and Sasha and I exchanged relieved glances.

"You really think we can?" she said.

Josh held up the plug with its twisty cable. "There's an old socket here," he said, tapping the wall. "Maybe the Enigma Machine can run off the mains. But we can't do anything if we haven't got power."

"Let me try." I eased the plug into the wall, half-expecting fiery sparks or some kind of an explosion.

Nothing happened.

"That socket must be part of a really old circuit," Sasha

sighed. "Maybe it just doesn't work any more."

"Press a key," suggested Josh. His eyes were much calmer now, shining.

I tapped down G and at the same time a letter C lit up in the middle panel.

My arm tingled. Josh leapt back with a cry. "Oh, excellent!" You could tell he couldn't wait to get his hands on it.

I pressed G again and a different letter, an R, lit up.

"Imagine how funny it will be when the Bletchley Park people find out there's a genuine Enigma Machine stuck behind a panel in the ballroom." Josh laughed. "*Initially you must set the three*," he read from the wall. "Lily could be talking about the key – you know – the three starting letters we have to set these dials to!"

Could Josh be right? And if we got the correct key, could we solve the whole of Lily's message?

I studied the three dials at the top of the machine, and the letters in the three windows alongside them: A—A—C. I'd noticed that the letter in the third window had changed as I'd typed; clicked one letter forward with each press.

"But the plug board needs to be set right as well," said Josh, pointing to the holes and wires we'd found when we'd swung the front wooden panel open. He peered at it. "At the moment it's set at . . . A to J, and . . . S to O. But your dad could have messed about with those; any curious thirteen-year-old would."

"Hang on." I'd had a thought. I lifted up Dad's loose page and flapped it at him and Sasha.

the settings when I found it

Josh grinned.

I checked the diagram quickly. "A to J, S to O. Good one! A—A—A. Put the key back to where it was!"

I didn't have to ask twice. Josh turned the right-hand dial on the Enigma Machine and the third letter went back to join the others: A—A—A.

The Enigma Machine was ready. Set exactly as Dad had found it. Exactly as Lily had left it?

"*Initially you must set the three!*" exclaimed Josh as the idea came to him. "A is the *initial* letter of the alphabet! The key *must* be right!"

"OK, then," I said, suddenly feeling all breathless. "Let's try."

"I've something to write with," said Sasha. She turned over Dad's paper and fished a pen from her pocket. "Ready," she said.

I shone one torch on the letters on the wall, and angled one on the Enigma Machine. "Go on then, Josh."

He took a big breath, then pressed the first letter from Lily's message. Q.

H lit up on the keyboard.

He pressed A, and another H came up.

Next came N and we got S.

A letter at a time, Josh typed the code from the wall while Sasha wrote down the letters as they lit up. We carried on, but it wasn't looking right at all. Sasha stopped and showed us what she'd written:

HHSDP. . . That didn't make any sense. What a let-down.

"The key must be wrong," Josh said, frowning. "We'll have to try another."

"Lily would have chosen a key that meant something, do you think?" I said. "Not just any old key, surely? Try . . . DAD."

"Good idea," Josh set the dials.

D—A—D.

The message still made no sense. That key must be wrong too.

"LIL, short for Lily?" suggested Sasha, tapping her pen on the page of the pad and looking doubtful.

L—I—L.

One-by-one she wrote down the lit-up letters.

Still nothing.

I racked my brain. "Try S—O—S."

Josh clicked the dials into place and I started to type. Another string of gobbledegook appeared on the pad.

"How did Bletchley Park ever work *any* messages out?" I said. "This is impossible! How many different keys are there, Josh? Can't we just try them all?"

"Just by a process of elimination? Well," said Josh. "It's quite a few. Usually with the extra rotors and different settings on the plug board there, there's. . ." He screwed

221

up his face. "A hundred and fifty-nine *million million million*."

I half laughed, half groaned.

"A hundred and fifty-nine quintillion for short," he added, like that made a helpful difference. "That's why the enemy thought their codes were uncrackable; that's why Bletchley Park needed Alan Turing's Bombes. You've a ten *million million* times better chance of winning the lottery than you have of guessing a key," said Josh. "Percy told me."

"Well, we've tried four settings," said Sasha, "so that's four down, and. . ." She wrote a number across the paper, then held it up with a crooked smile. "Only this many to go."

158,999,999,999,999,999,996

Million, million, million.

I thought about the pages and pages of crossed-out letters in Lily's notebook. She'd only had the Enigma Machine in here, no Bombe. She'd been trying to work out the keys for the messages she wanted to crack! Must have been.

Million, million, million. I thought about Lily, afraid, alone, crouched over the Enigma Machine in this little secret space behind the panels. Lily desperate to find out if Coventry was the target city in the Moonlight Sonata raid; desperate to decode an Enigma message that might tell her if it was. Lily gone a bit crazy, trying the keys and crossing them off one by one in her notebook. I heard the sound of keys clacking, a pencil being sharpened; saw the curls of wood shavings falling to the floor. Lily, exhausted, ill, trying to save her dad, trying to crack the dead duck codes she never would.

She hadn't deserved what happened to her, or what people said about her. "Initially you must set the three." I muttered the words under my breath, like a prayer. "Initially you must set the three."

Think literally and laterally, Nat. Literally and laterally.

Initially. An idea shot through me. Was the clue cryptic, like Josh had thought? A clue within a clue? *Initially.* Not the initial letter of the alphabet, but. . . My heart hammered.

Initials! Might the key be Lily's initials? "Hold the torches for me, Josh." I hurried to set the dials, forcing myself to remember her full name from the old address book.

Lilian Elizabeth Kenley.

L—E—K.

20

Cracking the Enigma Code

I clicked the three stiff dials into place, Josh trying to keep the torch beams still as he twitched with excitement.

L—E—K.

My fingertips hovered over the keys as I squinted at the code scratched on the wall and my fingers clumsily started to type. One by one the letters lit on the middle keyboard and Sasha scribbled them down, torchlight spilling across the page.

LILYKENLEYNOV

"*Yes!*" I hissed, punching the air with the fist of my good arm. The torch beams danced about as Josh jumped up and down, and Sasha hugged me tight.

EMBERNMETE

The string of letters were making words.

ENFORTYONEDAYIDLIKETOTH

Words with no spaces.

MKTHEYLLKNOWTHETRUTH

But words that made sense.

IAMATRAITORISTOLEAHENIGMACHMEIMADECO

I stopped, ears pricked, and I felt Sasha and Josh tense up.

There had been a sound. A sound from the place we'd come through. The sound of the panel sliding up, very, very slowly. Then a pause. I felt Josh holding my shoulder, really, really tight.

"Nathan?" A voice. Muffled and distorted through the narrow gap.

The panel slid up a little more. "Na-than." The voice again.

"They know we're here!" Josh said desperately, fumbling to switch off the torches. His mouth gaped and for a second before the lights went off, he looked ghost white, like one of the faces from the ballroom ceiling.

Dad's phone! I crammed it deep in the pocket of my jeans, squashing it against the bottle of perfume Sasha had brought for Mum.

We sat absolutely still. We knew we were trapped in there, that there was no other way out. The panel slid up a little more and a grey slab of moonlight reached towards us like a long, thick finger. Josh let out a horrified groan. I felt Sasha squeeze my arm so it was killing me. An eye was in the gap, looking straight at us.

"Nathan, is that you?"

Rose?

It *was* Rose, PhD Rose from the Bletchley archives room, her sparkly hat winking and her long blonde hair touching the floor as she leaned in. She shone her torch around. "What on earth are you doing here? What *is* this place? It's amazing!"

Sasha's voice was all suspicious. "What are *you* doing here?"

"I told you, I work through the night sometimes. I saw your light. Then heard you through the panels."

"There were people after us," blurted Josh. "We only just got through the gate in time! You should get in here with us – it's dangerous out there!"

Rose widened her eyes. "Are you sure? I didn't see anyone else."

"But what's going on? What are *you* doing here? What is this place?"

"It's too long to explain now," Josh said. "We can't let them find us, Rose, so get in here quickly, can you? We have to close the panel again and. . ."

"This place is amazing," she said again. She sat cross-legged in the gap, peering in.

The three of us exchanged looks. Had Rose heard Josh? Was she deliberately ignoring what I'd said?

"Best get home, I think," Rose said. "That's the safest thing. I can drive you, if you like. Take you back to Foxglove Cottage, Nathan."

My back stiffened against the shredded wall. "How do you know?" I said quietly.

"What?" said Rose, smiling at me, all innocent.

"How do you know I live at Foxglove Cottage?"

21
Traitor

Rose gave a short laugh. "You told me."

"No I didn't."

I saw Sasha and Josh's reaction, the way they'd started edging further away from where Rose was sitting. Tension shot through the secret room like a bullet.

I felt my mouth drop open. Rose. It all made sense suddenly. Appearing at Bletchley Park like that in just the right place at just the right time; Percy looking confused when her name was mentioned. All stuff we should have given way more thought to before. Rose knew I lived at Foxglove Cottage. Was *she* the one who'd broken into our house and been rifling around?

"Silly me," said Rose. All the friendliness had gone from her voice. She was filling the gap, blocking our escape.

"What do you want?" I said.

Rose's mouth set into a hard line. "Your dad made some sort of treasure hunt to find it, didn't he?"

I said nothing.

"I know about the evidence, Nathan," she said. "I heard you talking in your garden, so it's best not to play games."

Had it been her in the garden that other time too, I asked myself, when I first found the eye symbol; her in the long coat and hat, outside Mr Edwards's office?

"Anyway," continued Rose, "I know the whole story from that essay you wrote for your friends."

What did she mean? Those pages of explanation I'd written for Sasha and Josh on my pad? We stared at each other. She couldn't have read those! I'd burnt the papers on the fire straight after!

Rose must have seen our confusion. "The impression of your pen went through to the next pages, Nathan," she said. "A quick computer scan with some special software was all it needed. I managed to read the majority of it."

"You broke into Nathan's house!" spat Sasha. "Why didn't you just stop him before, then, while you had the chance?"

"I needed Nathan to follow the trail for me, of course," Rose answered, her voice calm and even. "Lead me to the evidence. Why else would I have helped you?"

I remembered our special treatment in the archive room; the nervous look the woman at the desk gave Rose as she flashed her pass – what had I seen on that pass again – an anchor. . .? Anchor, crown, eagle – would that have been the emblem for the Ministry of Defence?

"You work with my dad?"

"A different department. The MoD is a big place."

"Were you following me?" I said.

"I had to find out what you were up to," said Rose. "Lend a helping hand if needed. If you hadn't had that brainwave to ring me at the gate, I would have just slipped in quietly after you. Your football stadium decoy was clever, but I wasn't about to fall for that."

"But your fake Mrs Atkinson stopped me going out!" I said. "So what you're saying doesn't make any sense."

"Mrs Atkinson?" Rose shook her head. "Oh, she's not with me. She's just a Special Services agent on official government business. No, I *wanted* you to leave the house. How else would you lead me to the end of the trail? Once I'd found a way in, I just followed your footprints. Then I got a call from Mr Edwards. He's got two children. You can't really blame him."

So Mr Edwards told her where we were! He *was* being blackmailed!

"Why did you send those texts?" I said, my voice going hoarse.

"I thought Lily was a real person at first," said Rose. "I thought she might know where the evidence was, and I was trying to get you to contact her. It was an easy mistake to make."

"You must be losing your touch," said Sasha. "They can't get traitors like they used to."

"Sorry, Nathan," stuttered Josh. "But the pigeon was all wonky and I just. . ."

"It's OK, Josh," I said gently. I felt my jaw go tight.

What was Rose-the-traitor going to do next?

"That's enough explanation, I think," she said. "Where's the evidence, Nathan? I know you must have it. I want you to hand it over to me."

None of us moved.

"I want the evidence, Nathan," repeated Rose. "It's better if you cooperate."

We still didn't move.

"The evidence, Nathan." I heard the edge in her voice. "*Now.*"

There was something in her hand; the gleam of metal. My jaw went rigid. Rose had a gun, and she was pointing it straight at me.

"It's over." She beckoned with her fingers. "Just hand me the evidence and I'll help you all get home. I can't really guarantee your safety otherwise, Nathan, or that of your friends."

What choice did I have? She had a gun. I'd promised myself I'd keep Sasha and Josh safe.

Slowly I eased Dad's phone from my pocket. I saw a brief flicker of surprise on Rose's face as she saw it. "A phone, is it? I guess that makes sense."

"Don't give it to her!" said Sasha, holding my arm. "*Don't*, Nathan!"

"No, don't," said Josh shakily. "It's the end for your dad if you do!"

Would Rose really shoot us? Could she *really* do that, murder children? I shoved the phone back in my pocket with the perfume bottle. I chewed my lip. Braced myself.

Rose sighed. She looked like she was working something out a moment. The end of the gun quivered slightly. Then she drew back from the gap. "I actually don't need the phone anyway," she said. "You can keep it."

Alarms went off in my head and Sasha frowned at me. I craned my neck to see what Rose was doing and I saw her pick up one of the jars the painters had left. She screwed open the top and sloshed the contents on the panels round us. A sharp acidic smell hit the back of my throat, the smell of turps or something, that stuff you use to clean paint off brushes. That really highly flammable stuff.

We started to scramble forward from the gap, but Rose swivelled the gun towards us. "Stay there, please."

I shunted back. Josh tugged his hair and put a hand over his mouth.

I knew suddenly what she was going to do. Destroy the phone; destroy the evidence. But just getting rid of the *evidence* wasn't enough, was it?

Us kids knew way too much.

It would look like an accident, I thought, panicking. The painters would get blamed most probably – they both smoked, didn't they? Or we'd get the blame. Three trespassing kids with stolen keys, found in the burnt-out ruin that was left. An arson stunt gone wrong.

"Why are you doing this?" said Sasha, her voice thick.

Rose's eyes were blank. "It's not just me," she said.

"There's a whole group of us, but then you knew that. Do you know the kind of power some of these people have?" For a second I saw a look in her face, something desperate; a look of someone in too deep? Her face switched back. "They know I'll finish the job."

Gun still pointed, she opened up more jars. "There're people in high places," she said, like she was talking half to herself. "People a lot more important than three kids. Things you wouldn't understand. Secrets." Turps and paint thinner splashed across the room. "Have you any idea how much secrets are worth? Secrets about soldiers' movements; military manoeuvres. Do you know what people will pay to get hold of that kind of information?" She laughed, a hard, bitter laugh. "How ironic to end up here, in Bletchley Park of all places! But people always did make good profit from war, whichever side they were on."

"Soldiers got killed because of what you did!" shouted Sasha.

"There are always casualties. Soldiers know the risks." With a sharp downward movement, Rose ripped the plastic off a velvet curtain and doused it with liquid from a bottle. "Leon Vane got too clever for his own good. He found out secrets were going missing and landed himself in it." She sloshed the liquid in a trail across the floor. "All this wood panelling," she said to herself. She kicked a plastic bucket, and brushes and rollers and foul-smelling sludge splatted across the floor. "A real fire hazard, and with the fire alarms I disconnected. . ."

Sasha was looking at me wild-eyed. Josh still had his hands over his mouth. She'd had this as an option all along, had she? Burn down the ballroom with us still in it.

"They must be paying you a lot," said Sasha. "Killing three kids!"

Rose lit a cigarette with a lighter, then snapped the lighter closed. She turned the cigarette between her fingers and gently blew the end. For a moment the orange glow lit her face, and for some reason I thought about the guy on the bonfire with his smiling mask. I had to think straight! I had to do something!

"There are always casualties," Rose said again, like she was programmed. But she didn't look at us as she said it.

I knelt there trembling, eyeing the glowing tip of the cigarette. I had to keep her talking. Had to buy time to think. . .

Think, Nat, think! Literally and laterally.

Memories swept through my mind like ghosts. I couldn't stop them – the memories of Dad and me poured through my head; everything the trail had made me remember. Bedtime stories and birthday breakfasts. Football matches and sweet hot chocolate. Me on Dad's shoulders so I was taller than anyone. Writing our names with sparklers, round and round, faster and brighter, in a fizzing spinning burning eye.

Suddenly I knew what I had to do. All at once, it was clear, like something magical, a secret code broken.

My fingers closed round the glass bottle in my pocket. *Keep calm and carry on.* I was edging the lid off with my fingertips.

I held Dad's phone out to Rose through the open panel. "Take it!" I shouted.

"Don't, Nathan!" Sasha cried. *"Please!"*

My other hand ran over the cold surface of the perfume bottle. I was using touch to align the nozzle. "It's over, Sasha," I told her. "It's not worth it."

My head turned so only her and Josh would see, and I winked.

There was a slight pause, but Sasha cottoned on fast. She narrowed her eyes, then shouted, "How can you *say* that? After everything we've been through? What's going to happen to your dad?"

"Take it," I pleaded, shifting towards Rose, hand outstretched, *"please.* Just let us go."

A bit of ash dropped from the tip of the cigarette. "It's too late for that now, I'm afraid."

"Please, Rose," I begged. *"Please."*

"But Nathan," called Josh in a fake whisper, "a fire might not completely destroy the phone. The computer chip inside could stay intact. I read an article that said the newest models are made with a special kind of heatproof plastic and. . ."

Rose seemed to take the bait. She looked unsure a moment, and you could see her calculating what might happen if anything on the phone turned out intact.

She looked annoyed. Keeping the gun in her hand, she balanced the smouldering cigarette on the edge of a nearby tin of paint and came forward to take the phone off me.

Keep calm. You need to get the timing exactly right. I held the phone just out of her reach. "Pass it," she said, her voice spiky with impatience. She crouched in front of us with the gun and her forehead glistened with sweat. *Closer. A little closer. . .*

Her face came near to us and I pressed the phone into her palm. "Sorry, kids," she said, her eyes blinking in the gap. "This is nothing personal." Then she started to slide the panel shut, and for a second the gun was pointing away from us and I saw my chance.

My

one

chance.

I whipped the perfume bottle out of my pocket and blasted the spray in her face as hard as I could. Rose reeled away with a cry, rubbing madly at her eyes. She staggered back, and the gun spun out of her hand, going off, and one of the fancy light shades on the ballroom ceiling shattered in an explosion of glass.

I squirmed out of the secret room. I saw her knock the paint can with her foot so the cigarette flipped up and made an orange arc towards the window. There was the smell of melting plastic, and flames snaked up a curtain. I stood there, staring. Rose tripped on a crinkled-up painter's sheet, her feet getting wound up in it. Her arms waved blindly to stop herself falling. She grabbed at the stepladder, making it lurch. Making the latch unhook again from its metal loop.

Sasha and Josh were beside me, about to run for the door, but I held their arms. "Get back behind the panel!" I told them. "The scaffolding's going to fall!"

"It's going to fall!" I shouted at Rose as I dived back towards the opening of the secret room and crouched there with Sasha and Josh.

The ladder swayed, then swung uncontrollably, and the scaffolding attached to the top of it started to swing too. There was an ear-splitting wail of metal under strain and hooks forced loose. The scaffolding was leaning, toppling, pieces of steel and wood shifting, tipping, crashing down. Screams echoed all around. Sasha's, Josh's. My own.

And then Rose was gone. Disappeared under the wreckage.

I stared as Dad's phone slid across the floor. It spun in the middle of the ballroom floor in the moonlight and I couldn't take my eyes off it. Round it went, round and round in graceful, shuddering circles, gradually slowing to a stop.

There was an eerie silence. Then the steady crackle of flames. I pulled myself together. I got out from the cramped space and ran over to scoop up the phone.

"Rose. . ." Josh panted by my ear. "Is she. . .?"

We looked at the pile of twisted metal and smashed wood.

"We have to go," I said.

"Yes, like *right now*!" coughed Sasha. *"Come on!"*

The stench of smoke was already filling the air and we raced for the ballroom door, but after Sasha and Josh had gone through, I paused.

The Enigma code in the secret room – it'd be destroyed and then we'd never be able to read Lily's message. I still had Sasha's phone in my pocket – I could use the camera to photograph it and. . .

"We have to go, Nathan!" Sasha was beside me again, tugging at my arm so I winced with pain. I pressed Dad's phone into her hand. "What are you *doing*?"

"You get out!" I shouted as I ran back across the ballroom floor. I saw the fire reach the curtain rail and spread along it. "Get out, *now*!" I pulled my scarf over my nose and mouth and ducked back into the secret room. I heard the flames spit and a sound like ripping wrapping paper as I desperately tried to take the photos I needed.

The smell of burning got stronger. Smoke began to coil through the secret room making my eyes sting, but I still hadn't photographed all the message. I doubled over, coughing and dropped the phone, the camera flash going off like a firework, blinding me. The flames got louder. The air crackled and gasped as I crawled around to find the phone. . .

Then there were other noises. Feet pounding across the wooden floor. A voice all high and giving orders – it couldn't be! I nearly stumbled over in surprise – *Hannah?*

Swearing. *Gavin?* There was a deafening hiss, then a rancid smell of fumes and foam and wet.

I came out of the secret room in a daze. The curtains still smoked, but the fire was out. Gavin stood there with a fire extinguisher and his mouth hanging open, and there was soot on his nose and his skull-and-crossbones jacket.

Then Hannah was there and she had hold of me, clutching me. "Nathan," she said. "*Nathan*," and my throat was all choked up, and then she was pulling me. "We're going somewhere safe."

Car headlights swung across the ballroom from outside, making our shadows glide like ghosts across the panels. I gripped Josh's arm and Sasha's hand and we gazed out of the window at the flashing blue light.

"My uncle's in the police," said Gavin, the first words he'd ever said to me. "So shift."

22
Nothing But the Truth

I'm up in the attic library, sitting stroking Bones, and I'm sitting by the window looking at the newspaper cuttings, remembering that night all those weeks ago.

TOP CIVIL SERVANTS ARRESTED FOR SELLING STATE SECRETS

and

INNOCENT MAN GOES FREE

Birds peck at old crusts of bread scattered on the lawn. I can hear Hannah laughing somewhere downstairs, my crazy big sister. Trust her to sneak a look in my wardrobe and find the Bletchley Park keys and the bike helmet and put two and two together. Rose hadn't been the only one good at eavesdropping, put it that way.

Hannah had put one of Mum's sleeping tablets in the fake Mrs Atkinson's cocoa. It turns out it was *Gavin's* car that went past us when we were on our bikes, complete with a pair of wire cutters in the boot.

More birds fly down and dodge between the others, looking for crumbs.

And while Gavin got talking to his policeman uncle and we were bundled off to a safe house, Hannah got using her journalist contacts and we forwarded the files of Dad's evidence, and it wasn't long before a load of newspaper people were parked outside the MoD.

The birds flap and hop in circles like they're dancing.

All the evidence we needed was right there, on Dad's phone. Everything. Dad *buying* information in the abandoned car park, not selling it. Photos of documents and video clips of the corrupt staff at their secret meetings. Computer logs that showed how they'd set Dad up. Taped conversations that proved *they* were guilty, not him.

Bones sprawls out on the old rug, the sun beaming in on him from the skylight, and gives a contented little yowl.

I still have bad dreams about the gun going off and the scaffolding collapsing, but Rose was OK in the end, just a couple of broken legs and a broken arm, and she confessed all from her hospital bed to get a lighter sentence, and so that pretty much sealed the prosecution's case.

The lawn is a mass of whirling wings.

It turns out it was true Dad realized his solicitor had been got at. When backup files of evidence he gave Mr

Edwards access to all disappeared, he knew he couldn't trust him.

So Dad had been forced into Plan B.

Messenger Bird.

Me.

Mum comes up and pops her head into the room. "Nearly ready for our walk?" she asks, and she smiles at me and then goes back down.

Carefully, I fold up the cuttings. Course, it was in all the papers. Miscarriages of justice make good headlines, and corrupt government people, and incredible happenings at Bletchley Park. Luckily Percy didn't seem too worried about his nicked keys or the singed curtains once we showed him the secret room and the Enigma Machine, though he did have to sit down while Josh fanned him with an information leaflet.

After all, apart from that soundproofing, we didn't break anything.

Only Lily's code.

Yeah, we finished Lily's message. Dad admitted it had taken him months to solve her trail when he was a kid, and he guessed I'd be stuck on the moon and star drawing and need some extra help there because that one took him weeks and weeks to crack.

Why had he never told me about the trail? It turns out he had been planning to, on my thirteenth birthday, because that's how old he was when he found Lily's first clue.

LILYKENLEYNOVEMBERNINETEENFORTYONE
DAYIDLIKETOTHINKTHEYLLKNOWTHETRUTH...

I look at the piece of paper in front of me where I'd
written out Lily's message from the secret room. In my
head I imagine her own voice, reading the words out
aloud.

Lily Kenley, November 1940
One day I'd like to think they'll know the
truth.
I am a traitor.
I stole an Enigma Machine. I made copies
of intercepts. I broke the code of silence
and compromised others.
But I refused to speak of any of this
at the time, for there were people who
helped me. Friends I had sworn to protect.
I'd made them also swear a promise never
to say a word.
So I laid a trail, of sufficient complexity
to hope my friends would stay protected
long enough. The truth can be a dangerous
thing.
I must write fast. I fear they will come
for me soon. I must tell and then hide my
story while I have time.
I pleaded with my father to get out of

242

Coventry, but he refused to act on what he called "a whim". After Mother died, and then my brother, he was so hard to reason with. There must be evidence, he told me, proper evidence, or he'd not believe it. But though I worked night after night in this secret room, I failed.

Yes, I am a traitor. I accept my fate, as any good traitor should.

But a traitor to whom? My country? My family? My friends? Myself? For what is loyalty? What if each of these loyalties is divided? Which one of country, family, friends, self is to be saved then?

My family are all dead. I do not care what happens to me. But I care that someone, one day, might follow the clues I laid and know the truth. That all I ever wanted was to save my father. This thought gives a little peace to my troubled mind.

I admit my guilt. I confess to all my crimes. And if loving someone too much is a crime, I confess to that as well.

A bird flies past through the skylight and Bones looks up and wags his tail, thumping dust off the rug.

The display board at Bletchley got changed.

BP'S INCREDIBLE SECRET the title says now.
HUT 6 WORKER GRANTED ROYAL PARDON

I put the cuttings back in their envelope and smooth the flap shut.

Do you believe in ghosts? I do. I believe in the past, anyway. How it can come back and touch you even after years and years. Is that what being haunted means?

Bones's muzzle twitches. I think about Lily in her prison cell, blaming herself and all alone. Only she wasn't alone, not really. She had people who cared about her. The people at Bletchley who helped her and she wanted to protect. Her landlady. Hilda. Dad, and now me.

I've put one of Auntie Hilda's old war medals on the windowsill for Lily, below the eye she etched. She might not have saved her own dad, but she helped me save mine.

I go downstairs and get my coat on and I go outside, and they're waiting for me in the garden, smiling: Mum and Hannah. And Dad.

We step into the woods, arm in arm, the four of us. Brother, sister, mother, father. Striding through the shadows and the sunlight, keeping walking on until we're hidden by the trees.

There was no Lily Kenley. There's no moonbeam in the ceiling; no secret room behind a shifting wooden panel of the Mansion ballroom (although you ought to visit Bletchley Park and check these things for yourself to be sure).

But there *were* griffins either side of the Mansion doorway the last time I looked, and during the Second World War there were real life code-breakers who were very, very good at keeping secrets. And so good at what they did that their work probably chopped *two whole years* off the War.

But once-upon-a-time there were plans to get rid of Bletchley Park. Plans to flatten the site; maybe one day build a supermarket and concrete it over with a car park. Luckily some people didn't like that idea. That couldn't be allowed to happen to somewhere so important, could it? So a few years ago a campaign was started, and the word began to spread, and the message travelled fast, and in July 2011 the Queen unveiled a memorial at Bletchley Park to honour the people who worked there, at last. In October 2011, funding was announced to continue restoring the site, including the precious, tumbledown Hut 6 I saw when I was first there. Which all goes to show just what can be done when there's something worth saving, and people who care enough about saving it.

Websites

Bletchley Park and the campaign to save it:
www.savingbletchleypark.org
www.bbc.co.uk/news/uk-14164529
www.adefoto.co.uk

> *"It is so important to communicate to our younger generation the important role that mathematicians played in saving this country of ours at its time of greatest danger."*
>
> Frank Jackson, Bletchley Park Volunteer

World War II and Enigma code:
www.en.wikibooks.org/wiki/Wikijunior:World_War_II/ Enigma

Write your own Enigma messages:
www.pbs.org/wgbh/nova/decoding

Support for families of people in prison:
www.pffs.org.uk
www.prisonersfamilies.org.uk

Acknowledgements

Many sincere thanks are due in the writing of this book.

To the entire team at Scholastic for their unstinting support. To my editor, Alice Swan, and Clare Argar, for keeping me on the right path. Jamie Gregory for the cover. To my agent, the marvellous Anne Dewe, wishing her a long, happy retirement.

To everyone at the inspirational Frederick Bird School, for the warmest of welcomes. To Mr Hinman at the archives who showed me files from the Coventry Blitz, and Janette who took me to see the roofless ruin of the cathedral and told me about the city's spirit of reconciliation.

To all the Clan. To Mapu, for discussions about perfume bottles and dodgy scaffolding, Sarah E, for a quiet place to think, and baby Leo for keeping things quiet. To Silvana and Aldo, Margaret and Paul, for tireless grandparent duties.

To Inge, who loves maths, and Marco, who loves stories. To Dawn and Morris for insights into an older draft, and the poshest fish and chips in Liverpool. Joy, who lives in another Foxglove Cottage, and Grandma Wilson, who told me about the art of winching barrage balloons during World War II. To the people who live round Bletchley, with apologies for terrible liberties taken with the setting. To Caro, Josie, Susie and Sarah who helped me break the code.

To Frank, a Bletchley Park volunteer, who explained to me how an Enigma Machine works; and to Tim, Harriet and Alistair who took me to BP despite the snow. To Sue Black for starting the campaign. To photojournalist, Ade Fishpool, for the DVD. To the wonderful Beryl Middleton, 85 years old, who told me how she signed the Official Secrets Act at 18 and what it was like to work in Hut 7.

To family and friends across Europe and beyond, who taught me that war is a terrible thing, no matter which side you end up on.

And to Max, Anna and Elena, for patience way beyond the call of duty, as I worked round the clock to try and crack it.